Dickie Larsen's Pumpkin

and other stories

Growing up in the 1950s

Geoff Carr

First printing: December 2025

Paperback ISBN 978-1-7641-5610-3

eBook ISBN 978-1-7641-5611-0

Hardback ISBN 978-1-7641-5612-7

A catalogue record for this work is available from the National Library of Australia

Distributed by Lightning Source Global

Contents

Dedication

To my wonderful Mum and Dad. Long gone but always remembered with love. The inspiration for this book.

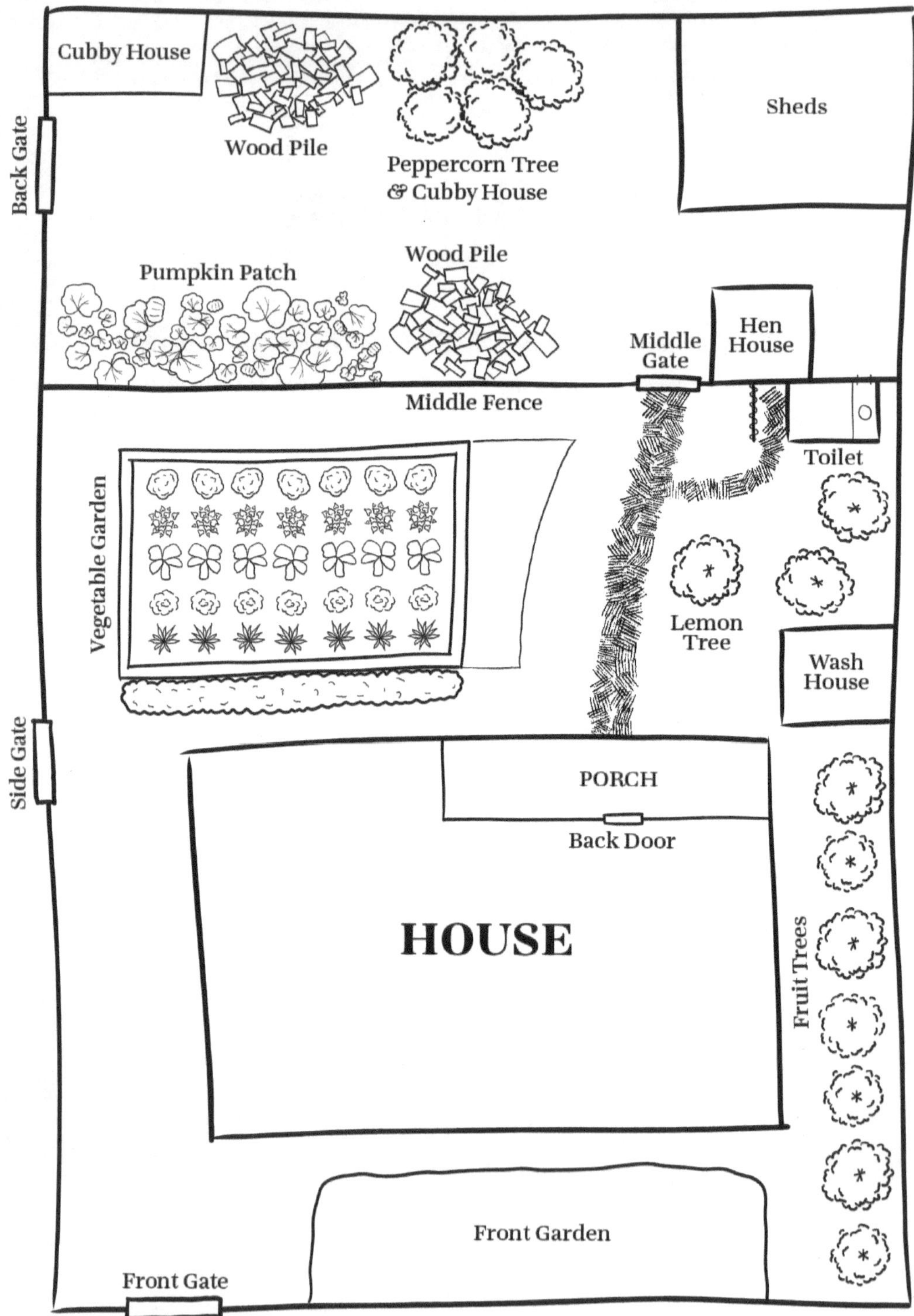
Cubby House
Back Gate
Wood Pile
Peppercorn Tree
& Cubby House
Sheds
Pumpkin Patch
Wood Pile
Middle Gate
Hen House
Middle Fence
Toilet
Vegetable Garden
Lemon Tree
Wash House
Side Gate
PORCH
Back Door
Fruit Trees
HOUSE
Front Garden
Front Gate

Foreword

Can you imagine living without televisions, washing machines, running hot water, refrigerators, mobile telephones (any telephones), toasters, flushing toilets, the internet, electric hotplates and ovens? You may not but there are still many who can. I remember it all clearly. The wireless, washhouse, hot water in a large kettle on the wood stove, a Coolgardie safe for cooling food, an ice chest (for the lucky ones) and a toilet down the garden path at a distance from the house. Younger generations would wonder how anyone could cope without the modern conveniences of today. But we did … and we did well. I spent my childhood during this time, and I have nothing but wonderful memories. Real incidents and experiences are the inspiration for these fictional stories. The main characters were my actual childhood schoolmates and cousins that I grew up with. Sadly, most have passed on. Older children today should enjoy my stories, but my writings should also stir memories of a life gone by in the older generations who, like me, lived in the 1950s. I hope young and old enjoy these stories.

The Fifties

Life was simple then.
Simple, but exciting and wholesome.
Dad went to work each day,
cut the wood,
grew vegetables and flowers.
Fed the chooks and the dogs and the ferrets
and had a drink every payday at the pub.
Mum stayed home
and happily cooked and cleaned and sewed.
She did the shopping every Thursday
and met the milkman and the butcher and the baker
at the back door each day and laughed and gossiped.
No luxuries.
Sometimes a struggle to make ends meet
but never a complaint.
I look back emotionally.
I think about my family, school friends and pets.
The bush.
Such peace and excitement and awe.
I loved the birds and animals, the trees and flowers,
the lakes and creeks, hills and mountains,
the large rocks and old mines.
Fishing and yabbying and rabbiting.
How I loved the bush and all it harboured.

But all that remains are vivid memories.
I cringe now at the intensity around me.
The hustle and bustle. Rush and worry.
Young minds, spinning with screens and buttons and keys.
Flashing lights, metallic sounds, synthetic din.

If only they would spend time in the bush.
If only they knew
what they were missing.

Old Rose

Our toilet seemed miles from the house. In fact, Uncle Ivan said that when he visited us, he always brought a cut lunch and a water bottle in case he needed to take the trip. It was built along the fence line dividing the backyard and the house yard. No sewerage in those days. Once a week, whether needed or not, a poor old man would come with an empty can and replace the full one. This old fellow was, of course, well known around town and because of the stench that usually accompanied him became affectionately known as Old Rose.

To enable Old Rose to accomplish the changeover, a small door was cut into the side wall of the toilet. The door was raised, the full can removed and the empty one placed beneath the hole in the toilet seat in readiness for the next week's offering. This door was on the wall, which was part of the middle fence, so that the poor old man had to go into the backyard and around the henhouse to change the can. I could never understand why anyone would want to lump those heavy, smelly tins around for a living.

Aunty Dot was big. Real big. When she walked her legs rubbed together all the way down to her ankles and her huge bottom and breasts floundered and wobbled like a monster jelly. Her head, though, was small and resembled a wrinkled onion. Dad said she was the only person he knew who carried an alligator-skin bag to match her complexion. As well, her eyes were always watery, and Dad said they'd fall out one day because the bottom lids hung down like those of a cocker spaniel. Her size was only surpassed by her ability to talk. She talked nonstop, an excited, high-pitched prattle. The amazing thing was that she didn't appear to stop for a breath. Dad said she breathed through her ears. Not many people liked Aunty Dot.

Unfortunately, Aunty Dot was coming from Melbourne to stay with us for a whole week. Dad was already in a bad mood and having to pick her up from the railway station only made him worse. She squeezed through the kitchen door, gave Mum an almighty hug, kissed me on the forehead, plonked herself on Dad's chair beside the wireless, took an almighty breath and started to talk.

And boy did she talk. She paused once, though, when she noticed me staring at one of her ears for signs of breathing.

"And have you got the sewerage on yet, love?" she asked Mum.

"No, not yet, but the plans can be viewed at the town hall. They say the first houses will be connected early next year."

"Oh, I suppose that means I still have to walk all that way down the back in the wind and rain to go to the toilet. You poor things. Fancy doing it all the time. It must be terrible, especially at nighttime."

"Oh, we have torches," said Mum.

"And does that same poor old man still carry that big, heavy tin around each week?"

"Old Rose? Yes, he's been doing it for many, many years now. Poor old fellow. He must be nearly due to be pensioned off." Mum sighed.

Aunty Dot immediately began her incessant ramblings again. Mum took refuge in the dinner dishes, Dad took off to fill the wood box and I pretended to be interested in the newspaper.

We had a holiday that Friday. The teachers had a conference. As usual, on holidays or Saturdays, my two friends would meet at my house and the day would be spent bird nesting or bottle collecting or rabbiting.

I heard the rattle of a bike on the outside of the tin fence and knew that Riddy had arrived. He was always early. A skinny, happy kid best known for the knitted green hat that he always wore. Leany arrived a few minutes later, his red face showing signs of exhaustion from the long ride up the steep hill between our two homes.

"I reckon we'll go rabbitin' today, Spike," said Riddy.

"Can't. Ferret's crook. Foot rot. Gotta rest 'im. Dad's put kero and sulfur on his feet."

"Looks like flippin' rain anyway," added Leany. "How about finishing the flippin' cubby in the peppercorn tree."

This bulky construction had been on the go for many months. Boards, bags, old lino and sheets of tin had been lugged up and roughly arranged to form a crude hut on the lower branches of the tree.

We figured that if we added more material to the roof, we could spend the rest of the day inside if it rained. And rain it did. Not heavy though, but a constant drizzle that annoys everyone. The cubby was quickly made waterproof and for a while we just sat around inside, talking about birds' eggs and foot rot.

Suddenly the back door of the house burst open and a huge figure emerged from the verandah. A large umbrella covered the shoulders and head.

"God, who's that?"

"Aunty Dot. She's off to the toilet."

"Hell, what a flippin' whopper."

"She'll soon fill it," said Riddy with a chuckle.

Aunty Dot glided down the brick path and disappeared around the creeper-covered trellis surrounding the front of the toilet.

"Remember the time we put the flippin' chook in the toilet?" Leany grinned.

"Yeah," replied Riddy. "Scared the hell out of Spike's mum. God, that was funny."

"Mum was pretty angry though. Wouldn't let me go to the pictures for two weeks."

Riddy was right – it had been hilarious. Just before Mum had reached the toilet, we bundled a chook through the little door in the toilet wall into the space where the pan sat. Just as Mum sat down, the chook panicked and started fluttering around beneath the seat. Mum nearly had a heart attack.

"Bet that fatso would run a mile if we did it to her," whispered Riddy, a fiendish glint in his eye. Leany's red face broke into a grin. They both looked at me.

"Hell no. Dad'll kill me."

"We'll do it," said Riddy. "Then ya won't get killed. Quick, before she's finished."

Before I could protest further, the two of them were scurrying down the trunk of the peppercorn tree. I decided it would be safer for me to stay where I was. The possibilities whirled through my mind. It would be worth walking a hundred miles to see what might happen. And besides, there was no better place to see the whole episode than from up in the tree house.

Riddy knew where to find a chook quickly. At this time of the morning, the nest boxes were full of hens laying the day's supply of eggs. He quickly entered the henhouse, picked up the nearest chook, came out with it tucked under his arm and, despite a few sharp pecks to his hand, disappeared in the direction of the toilet wall.

A lot happened in the next few minutes. Riddy gingerly lifted the square door on the toilet wall and silently shoved the chook into the dark space beneath Aunty Dot's bottom. The two boys then made a dash back to the safety of the cubby and settled down beside me to watch the fun. Our eyes and ears were riveted on the toilet door. Riddy was shaking with excitement. Our concentration was interrupted by a van pulling up at the side gate.

"Hell, it's the butcher."

Mr Newton jumped from the old dark-blue van carrying

a small white parcel, opened the gate and strode quickly to our back door.

"Butcha," he roared.

"Sour old rat," whispered Riddy. "Never seen 'im smile."

Mr Newton was not an old man, but he was as bald as a billiard ball and was known throughout the town as Marblehead. His father had been a butcher and his grandfather too.

Mum came to the door and the two of them engaged in their usual discussion about the weather or yesterday's meat.

We glanced back to the toilet. Surprisingly, it was calm.

"Perhaps the flippin' chooks died of fright," whispered Leany.

Suddenly I heard another vehicle chugging up the road and turned in horror to see a familiar green tray truck grind to a halt behind the butcher's van.

"My god, it's Old Rose."

Riddy and Leany looked uneasily at each other and then at me and then back to the toilet.

I could see my life flashing before my eyes. I knew something terrible was about to happen.

"Quick, get the chook," I squawked.

"Hell no, I'm not goin'," answered Riddy.

Leany shook his head. "Too flippin' dangerous. Anyway, it's too late now."

He was right. Rose, carrying the empty can on his padded shoulder, was trudging down the path to the middle gate. His big, heavy boots crunched on the stones scattered on the brickwork.

Mum and Marblehead glanced his way. Mum smiled but the old man remained stone faced, his eyes glued on the path before him. He lumbered through the gate and disappeared around the corner of the henhouse towards the little door in the toilet wall.

I've often wondered what Aunty Dot did when Rose opened the door, pulled out the full pan and shoved the empty one in its place. The chook too must have sat out the action in a corner of the dark cavity.

Anyway, while we watched from the cubby, we heard the door slam shut and the old man groan as he lifted the heavy pan onto his shoulder. He reappeared around the corner and struggled with one hand to undo the latch on the gate. He lurched through, stood precariously on one leg, kicked the gate shut with his huge boot and laboured back up the path.

Mum and Mr Newton were still swapping pleasantries when the toilet erupted. Apparently, the chook had had enough of sitting timidly in the dark, and just as Aunty Dot began to lift her huge bottom from the seat, it made a dash for the light coming from the now partly uncovered hole. It crashed, squawking and fluttering into Aunty Dot's bare bum and fell flapping into the empty pan.

Aunty Dot thought the gremlins had got her and, with her monstrous knickers still down around her ankles, shot out like a wounded hippo from the toilet. The chook scrambled up again through the hole in the seat and only made matters worse by fluttering after the terrified figure and beating its wings against her bare legs.

Mum, Marblehead and Old Rose all stopped in their tracks and stood stunned as Aunty Dot and the chook, who unfortunately by now had its leg caught in the elastic of the billowing bloomers, scrambled up the path towards the house. She was heading blindly towards the back door, and her huge frame, combined with the amazing speed she had attained, meant that anything in her path was a goner.

Rose saw her coming and made a valiant attempt to sidestep out of her path. However, whether it was his big, heavy boots or the weight of the pan on his shoulders, he just didn't seem to be able to move as quickly as he wanted.

We watched with horror as the two figures and the chook crashed head on and, amid flaying arms and legs, subsided in a heap beside the lemon tree. The old man, aware of the lethal weapon he was carrying, inwardly panicked. With the grace of a professional ballet dancer, he attempted to nurse the full pan to the ground without losing the contents. But all in vain. The lid burst open and the disgusting, smelly brew erupted and covered the three prostrate figures in a layer of slop too horrible to describe.

Aunty Dot rose to a kneeling position, her face locked in a

silent scream. Things were dropping and dripping from her as she crawled towards the house. Poor Old Rose lay stunned. He was still clutching the empty pan, which was resting on his chest. It rose and sank again each time he gasped for fresh air. The chook, all wet and bedraggled, its white feathers permanently stained, skulked off and hid in the rhubarb patch.

Mum stood frozen to the spot, unable to comprehend what had happened. Marblehead, for the first time in his life, saw the funny side of something and was bent over the rocking chair choking and coughing in his attempt to control his laughing. His face was crimson and his cheeks wet with tears.

Leany and Riddy remained silent until they turned to look at each other and then exploded in a state of hysteria. Both were on their knees, and between each raucous outburst of laughter, they would glance through the cracks of the cubby and immediately slump to the floor in another fit of coughing and spluttering.

I was mortified. I wondered how long I could hide in the cubby without food. Finally, Riddy looked up at me from the floor. Between his chokes and gasps, he garbled something about "chook" and "knickers" but then sank slowly again to the floor, rolled onto his back and lay there panting and twitching.

The whole episode certainly had its effect from that day on. Every time Marblehead pulled up at the side gate, he was grinning from ear to ear. He was known to burst out laughing on the most sombre occasions. Old Rose never recovered from his terrible ordeal. His eyes, once glued to the ground in front of him, darted around in a frenzied search for any movement as he detoured the lemon tree.

Dad drove a surprisingly quiet and subdued Aunty Dot to the railway station the next day. He was in a good mood and, despite the previous day's turmoil, was whistling softly between his teeth. Just before they headed for the railway station five days earlier than intended, he leant down and whispered in my ear.

"I hope that chook's still around next time she comes."

Gladiata

Everybody around town thought that old Mrs Snipe was a bit queer.

She'd lived on her own for most of her life in a small, ramshackle old house held together by a thick layer of ivy. The ivy had for many years crept and entwined itself around the walls, roof and chimney until only the doors and some of the windows of the shack were visible. The areas around the house were littered with piles of rusted drums, old beds, bottles, tins, jars, broken machinery, dead trees and a couple of dilapidated drays that hadn't been moved for many years. A few skinny chooks wandered around in the junk and dust and a black, wild-eyed dog chained to one of the dray wheels kept watch over the whole uninviting mess.

The house stood out like Granny's tooth in the middle of a dry, barren paddock. An almost unused track wound its way from a wooden gate near the road to the old house. The old, rusted hinges of the gate were attached to thick rotting posts and creaked every time it was pushed open. This paddock was the home for nearly one hundred goats. Goats of all sizes and colours roamed the arid paddock searching for something to eat. Many of them trudged continually around a fenced-off haystack, no doubt wishing they could get at the bales of hay packed under a crude corrugated iron roof.

"Ever seen old Snipey?" asked Leany as we rode our bikes past the paddock one morning.

"Yeah," I answered. "Looks like one of the goats. Beard n' all."

Just as we rode slowly past the old wooden gate, a tiny, hunched figure wrapped in an old, tattered brown coat and knitted grey scarf strutted from a hole in the ivy and headed for the haystack to feed the goats. The goats immediately stampeded towards the hurrying figure, who was obviously intent on reaching the haystack fence before they did. She slid through the strands of wire just as the goats scrambled and scrunched to a halt behind her. They jostled and struggled for front positions and bleated and butted and fought until the milling mass gradually disappeared in a huge cloud of swirling orange dust. A few bundles of hay suddenly flew through the air and disappeared in turn into the middle of the turmoil. After a moment, the little hunched figure emerged from the dust, glanced back at the brawling goats and then headed back to the ivy. Just as she was about to disappear into the shack, she turned and saw us watching from the side of the road.

"Get outta here," she screeched, waving her arms in the air. "Don't want none of you brats around here. Don't want you teasin' m'goats. Get outta here before I let m'dog loose."

She took a couple of steps towards the snarling black dog and then stopped as she saw us jump reluctantly on our bikes and pedal off down the road.

"Ya old witch," roared back Riddy. He made a rude sign with his hand and we all laughed as old Snipey grabbed a stick and flung it in our direction.

"Stupid old coot," yelled Riddy. "Mad as a meat axe."

He was about to yell more but changed his mind as the little old figure disappeared in the ivy.

"What does she do with all those flippin' goats anyway?" asked Leany as we struggled up the hill towards town.

"Sells 'em, I s'pose," answered Riddy.

"Dad says she eats 'em," I said.

"Goats?"

"Yeah. He says young ones are okay. Bit like lamb."

"Hell. No wonder she looks like one." Riddy grinned. "Fancy eatin' 'em. Yuck."

"Dad said that when he was a kid they used to race 'em. Stick little carts behind 'em. He said they could really go."

"How's the cart tied to the goat?" asked Riddy.

"Blowed if I know," I answered. "I'll ask Dad when I get home."

Dad was out weeding his carrots when we dropped our bikes against the tin fence and marched down to where he was kneeling on the ground.

"Dad, you know those racin' goats you were tellin' me about the other night? How did you tie 'em to the carts?"

"That was a long time ago," grunted Dad. "Can't remember much about it. I think we made a rope noose and put it around the goat's neck. The shafts of the cart were tied to it. Why?"

"Oh, nothing," I mumbled. "Just wondering," I continued, trying not to sound too eager.

"What'd the cart look like?" asked Riddy.

"Just a box with a couple of wheels and two long, strong shafts," replied Dad, appearing to show some sudden interest in the conversation. "Bit like one of them roman chariots," he went on. He stopped weeding and stared at the ground. "Used to have races every Sunday morning," he pondered. "Betting and all. We'd have heats first. Then the final. Used to race 'em down a narrow lane. Pretty hard to steer though. Lots of crashes. I got a few bruises, I can tell ya. Ya Uncle Ron broke his arm once."

"Where'd ya get the goats from?" Riddy broke in.

"Most people had a goat or two in those days. Kept 'em for milk or used them as lawn mowers. Some people used to eat 'em."

"Yeah, we know," said Leany, screwing up his face and glancing at me.

Dad flinched and went back to his weeding.

"Anyway," he said, "thing of the past. Never hear of goat racin' nowadays."

He again stopped weeding and stared at the ground, a hint of excitement shining in his eyes. He was lost in thought and didn't notice our departure to our cubby in the peppercorn tree.

"Wish we could have a goat race," said Leany thoughtfully. "Must've been top fun."

"Yeah, we could make the carts all right, but gettin' the goats would be tough. Whose got 'em besides old Snipey? They'd have to be pretty tame. Wild ones would be no good. Hell, you'd get killed," said Riddy.

"I reckon old Snipey's goats would be pretty quiet. Look at the way they chase after her. They follow us along the fence when we ride past. If they were wild, they'd run the other way, wouldn't they," I said.

"Yeah, but they're starving. They'd follow anybody for a flippin' feed," answered Leany.

"Anyway, the old witch is nearly always home. We'd never get a chance to get near the goats let alone stick a cart on 'em and race 'em," went on Riddy.

"She rides her bike into town once a week to get her groceries. Takes her all morning. We could catch a couple of goats then," I suggested. "Won't take long to hitch 'em up and race 'em."

"Who are we going to race?" asked Riddy. "Can't race ourselves. Too much work. One cart will do us."

"What about Snake and his gang? They're always lookin' for something exciting to do. Bet they'd be in it."

Snake was in grade six at school. He was not over intelligent but nevertheless quite cunning and held in high esteem because of his sporting ability and daredevil attitude to life. He was a tall, skinny kid with penetrating blue eyes and long, wispy hair hanging over his ears and eyes.

"Goat race? How do ya do that?" asked a somewhat puzzled Snake after school the next day. We explained in pretty simple terms what it was all about, and Snake appeared quite excited until he heard the word Snipey.

"Hell no. Not goin' there. She's nuts. Sooled her dog onta me once. Grabbed me by the leg and pulled me off m'bike. Thought it was gonna eat me. Sniff here donged it on the noggin' with one of his rabbit traps and we got away. Not goin' back there."

Sniff nodded. "W-w-w-we only g-g-givin' her goats some g-g-grass through the f-f-fence." Sniff was a stuttering, nervous-like bloke with huge ears sticking from his head like table tennis bats. "N-n-n-not goin' back there," he echoed. "She's n-n-nuts."

"But she's never there on Wednesday mornings. Rides her bike into town to do her shoppin'. We can wag school. She wouldn't even know we'd been there. We just wait until she goes. Plenty of time. Only take us half an hour. She's away all morning," I said, trying to sound as confident as I could.

Snake looked at Sniff and back to me. "No thanks," he said. "Not worth the chance." He turned, signaled to Sniff and the two of them began to walk away.

"Scared, are ya?" snapped Riddy.

Snake stopped dead in his tracks and turned to face Riddy, a menacing scowl on his face.

"Me, scared? You've gotta be jokin'."

"Then why won't ya race us?" jeered Leany. "Bet ya ten bob ya can't beat us."

Snake looked at Sniff and smiled. "Ten bob, eh," he murmured. "Okay, ya on."

After a brief discussion about the rules and specifications for the big event, Snake and Sniff went home and we took off for our cubby in the peppercorn tree.

"Gotta build a cart. We'll get one of ya dad's bee boxes," said Riddy. "They're real strong. And two wheels. I'll get them off my cousin's old trike. They're fairly big. Just what we want. He won't miss 'em."

"Yeah, gotta have good wheels," I urged. "That's the most important part. We've gotta win the race."

"Where do we get the ten bob from if we don't?" queried Leany.

"Blowed if I know," replied Riddy rather irritably. "It was your idea. You find it."

"Hell, I haven't got ten bob," whined Leany. "You'll have to help."

"Let's worry about that later," I said. "Anyway, we won't lose."

The cart was made the next day. We stood admiring the orange speed machine.

"What'll we call it?" asked Leany.

"Something Roman-ish, I reckon," answered Riddy.

We looked at each other and thought hard.

"I know!" I yelled at last. "The Gladiator!"

"Yeah, pulled by Billy the Kid!" Riddy laughed.

"We'll paint the name on the cart."

I ran and got some black paint and an old brush from the cupboard in the washhouse.

"How do ya spell it?" asked Riddy, grabbing the paint and brush from me.

"Not sure. Put what ya think."

Riddy began to write the word in large black letters.

G L A D ... He paused and thought, repeating the word over and over to himself. He quickly added an I and finished with A T A.

"Yeah, that looks right," I said.

Leany wasn't so sure. "Should have double D," he said. "It doesn't seem right."

"It'll do," snapped Riddy. "Snake and Sniff won't have a clue whether it's right or wrong anyway."

The Gladiata was pulled into the woodshed and covered by two wheat bags. We didn't want Snake copying our design.

Wednesday morning came slowly. We had arranged to meet at half past nine in the bush beside Mrs Snipe's paddock. We would wait until we saw her set off for town and then try to catch our goats and hitch them to the carts.

We had agreed that I would drive the Gladiata and was suitably dressed in a pair of Leany's old blue overalls, Riddy's knitted green gloves that would help me grasp the rope reins and my black footy boots for extra grip on the floor of the cart. But when Snake and Sniff arrived, we stared in amazement. Sniff had obviously been talked into driving their cart and came fearing the worst. On his head he wore an old air pilot's leather helmet. Two holes had been cut in the sides and from them his huge pale ears stuck out at right angles from the black leather. His skinny arms and upper body were covered in layers of jumpers and his legs were protected by a pair of patched cricket pads. They were far too big and when he walked he clutched the tops so that they didn't slip off. To complement the pads, he had a pair of cricket gloves, believing as we had that they would improve the grip on the reins.

But that wasn't all. The cart was a work of art. Somehow Snake had cut down a forty-four-gallon drum into the shape of a true Roman chariot and two steel shafts had been welded to the side of it. Two huge bike wheels dominated the design. The whole chariot had been painted black and we stood and stared in awe.

"Strewth," whispered Riddy. "Take a gander at that."

Snake was grinning proudly. "Me and m'dad made it. Not

bad, eh. Copied it out of one of them history books. Just like the real one."

Sniff nodded. "Y-y-y-yeah. J-j-j-just like r-r-r-r-r …" His nerves suddenly got the better of him and he decided not to finish the sentence.

By this stage quite a crowd of onlookers had gathered around the two carts.

"Got that ten bob?" jeered Snake. "Ya won't win in that cart." He knelt beside his chariot and dripped some oil from a can onto the hubs of the huge wheels. "Ya won't see us for dust. Will they, Sniff?"

Sniff nodded. He hadn't moved far from where he stood from the moment he arrived. Walking was difficult. He swallowed hard and tried to grin. "M-m-m-might be best if y-y-y-you drive, S-S-S-Snake."

"Don't be stupid. I'm too heavy. You're real light, Sniff. Just what the doctor ordered."

Sniff flinched nervously when the word doctor was mentioned and, still clutching his cricket pads, shuffled over and stood beside Snake. Just then one of the onlookers noticed some movement at the tumbledown house.

"Shut up. Here comes Snipey."

Old Mrs Snipe grabbed her bike, which was leaning against the ivy, jumped on and sped surprisingly quickly down the track. When she reached the old wooden gate, she opened it, slipped through and shut it all in the twinkling of an eye. The goats spotted her and stampeded down the hill towards the gate in the hope of a feed. But by the time they got there, Snipey was peddling down the road and heading to town.

"Right. Let's go," cried Snake, and the whole show emerged from the trees and bushes and congregated along the wire fence bordering Mrs Snipe's paddock. The goats, having lost interest at the wooden gate, immediately headed in our direction.

"Quick!" yelled someone. "Get some grass and let's catch a couple."

"Get two big 'uns. They'll run faster."

Sniff flinched again. The audience divided themselves into two groups and crept through the fence towards the goats. The goats appeared a little nervous but, encouraged by the handfuls of grass, stood where they were and allowed themselves to be fed and patted.

"Those two there," said Snake softly, nodding towards a pair of the biggest goats in the herd. "When I give the word, grab 'em."

The two groups of boys manoeuvred their way slowly to the unsuspecting pair. The goats munched on the grass.

"Now!" yelled Snake.

Immediately, the two goats were grabbed from all angles. They bucked and reefed and tried to butt their captors but were held tightly by the sheer weight of numbers. Sensing the danger, the rest of the goats took off in a cloud of dust to the far end of the paddock and stood there twitching and staring in our direction. The two goats were dragged over to where the two carts had been lifted over the fence.

"Put the loops over their heads. Tie the rope to the shafts," puffed Riddy.

While the goats stamped and snorted, they were harnessed and dragged around until they were both pointing in the same direction.

"Round the haystack and back," cried Snake. "Come on, Sniff, get in quick."

Sniff looked reluctantly at Snake and then at the goat. He

was about to say something but immediately found himself being lifted into the chariot by eager pairs of hands. I climbed into the bee box, grabbed the reins tightly and braced myself in a kneeling position against the walls of the cart. The goat, still held tightly by half a dozen helpers, thrashed and stamped. Two boys had a vice-like grip on the horns but were having a great deal of trouble holding the goat steady.

Sniff was petrified.

"Stand up, Sniff," yelled Snake, "or ya won't be able to see over the front of the cart. Got ya whip?"

Sniff fumbled around the floor of the chariot and held up a thin stick with a small leather strap attached to the end. "Y-y-y-yeah," he stuttered.

"Okay," yelled Riddy, appointing himself the official starter. "Get ready."

The crowd hushed.

"Go!"

The boys holding the two goats let go and fled to the fence. The crowd roared but the goats didn't move. They just stood there.

"What's wrong with 'em?" whined a voice.

"Probably too scared to run," said another.

"Whack it with ya whip, Sniff," Snake called out.

Sniff very gently lifted the whip and touched the goat on the rump with it. Nothing happened.

"Hard, you idiot!" roared Snake.

Sniff shut his eyes and whacked. That did the trick. The goat immediately flew three feet in the air and shot off like a bullet across the paddock. Mine, not to be outdone, nearly jerked the reins out of my gloved hands as it cannoned forward in an attempt to stay with the first. Through the whistling of the wind, I could hear Sniff screaming.

"They're goin' the wrong flippin' way," yelled Leany.

"Steer it, ya idiot," roared Snake.

But Sniff's only thought was to remain in the cart. I was a bit worried too. There was no way the goats were going to respond to the reins. Now I knew why Dad raced them down a narrow lane. To make matters worse, the paddock was not all that smooth and Sniff in particular was having a dickens of a time trying to remain in the cart. At each bump he shot into the air and landed with a bang on the metal floor of the drum. This only frightened the goat more and as it ran it bucked and butted and swerved across the dust. This made the ride most terrifying for Sniff and he suddenly threw caution to the wind, let go of the reins and dropped to the floor.

The group of onlookers were beside themselves with excitement. This was more than they had bargained for.

The two goats bolted towards the rest of the herd cowering in the far corner of the paddock. But when the carts came bouncing at them, they took off along the front fence, passed the rickety wooden gate and crowded and crushed themselves in the other corner of the paddock. The two chariots wheeled in a half circle and took off after them.

Unfortunately, it was during this dash that things got a little out of hand. At this point, the two goats and their carts were speeding along side by side. I could see Sniff's back and leather helmet hugging the floor. He was bouncing around in the drum. His screams had subsided to a few sharp yells of pain as he hit the walls and floor of the cart.

I thought perhaps I might be able to slow the goats down if I was able to grab the shaft of Sniff's chariot. I reached out but this only caused the two of them to veer sideways and hit the old wooden gate on the way past. The gate tottered for a few seconds and then crashed to the ground in a swirl of dust. At the same time, the wheel of my cart slammed into a small stump and I was thrown high in the air. I landed, skidding and bouncing on the hard, dry ground. I lay there stunned. My chest hurt. I couldn't breathe properly. My nose was bleeding. There were big holes in the knees of my overalls.

A few of the boys watching came running down past the goats to my aid. But this only frightened the herd once more and they again took off along the front fence with Sniff still in tow.

"They're heading for the gate!" yelled Snake. "They'll get out. Stop 'em. Quick!"

But it was too late. The goats streamed out of the paddock. However, they quickly stopped along the side of the road when they saw the grass growing in large clumps under the trees. But

Sniff's goat wasn't interested in grass. Although appearing very tired and terrified, it took off along the road and up the hill to town.

Old Butsy Jones had died two days earlier of a heart complaint. He was a popular old stick and a large gathering had congregated at the local cemetery to see him off. The sombre crowd was standing silently and the minister was praying and sprinkling dirt on the coffin deep in the grave.

"Ashes to ashes. Dust to dust," warbled the minister.

He lifted his ashen face and slowly raised his arms towards the heavens in an impressive show of divinity. And then he remained in silence. The mourners, aware of the long pause, looked up and turned to see what had captured his attention. A goat pulling a black cart was rattling and bumping up the gravel track towards them.

"It's coming straight for us," croaked a voice.

"Quick, get out of the way. It's really moving!"

The crowd scuttled in all directions as the goat swerved and bucked its way through the mass of black suits and dark dresses. It threaded its way between legs, occasionally knocking some poor old unfortunate flat in the dust, and shot up the little slope towards the open grave. The minister remained there motionless, his arms still raised towards God. Suddenly he realised he was in danger and made a valiant attempt to jump clear of the rushing goat. But he left his run a little late and was collected by the onslaught and was hurtled screaming into the hole where the coffin lay. The goat tried desperately to jump the gaping hole and but for the cart would have made it. The crowd of shocked mourners rushed to the grave as the goat, clawing and scrabbling at the walls of the grave, slowly disappeared from sight to join the unfortunate minister.

The whole scene froze for a full minute until two cricket gloves and a shiny black head slowly appeared from the depths. A white, wide-eyed creature stared in shock at the equally stunned onlookers.

"What is it?" someone whispered.

"Where'd it come from?"

A few of the braver mourners crept to the edge of the grave and helped the oddly clothed creature from the hole. Next to appear was the minister, who was helped to the hearse by some of his flock and sat there trembling and shaking his head as he clutched his Bible. No one was game enough to get into the grave to rescue the goat and it was left to a couple of grave diggers that night to relieve Butsy of his hairy companion.

On the following Saturday, the local newspaper ran the story of the goat race on the front page. A large picture of Sniff standing beside the chariot and sporting a few bruises and band-aids was the dominating feature. He became an immediate hero to the kids at school and was patted on the back and asked repeatedly to retell his version of the story. Old Mrs Snipe's goats were rounded up over a day or two and locked away behind a quickly erected brand-new steel gate.

Dad read the account of the incident, occasionally glancing at me and shaking his head in disbelief.

"My god," he muttered. "Goat racing. What will kids today think of next."

The Tree Had to Go!

At the far end of our schoolyard was a group of about a dozen large pine trees surrounding one huge gum tree, which had obviously been there for hundreds of years, even before the school had been built. But over the past few months, a couple of large dead branches had fallen off. Luckily, they fell during the school holidays or over the weekends when the yard was deserted. But the school council became worried that another limb could fall and a student or two could be injured or, worse still, killed. So, they declared that the tree had to go. It was far too big a job for the council or parents to achieve, so word went out through the local newspaper asking for anyone who had the knowledge, experience and equipment to cut down the huge tree and to remove the stump and the roots. The school council would cut up the tree once it was down and sell it as firewood, with the proceeds going back to the school.

A few enthusiastic and hopeful souls applied for the job and finally the task of cutting down the tree was awarded to two middle-aged woodsmen nicknamed Mantis and Sticka. If you ever saw the two of them, you would know why. Neither had an ounce of fat on them and were all elbows and legs. Dad said you could use them as goalposts!

The following week, the two tree experts arrived to survey the situation. They stared at the tree for some time, walked continually around it, tapped it again, estimated the height and stood studying it. They were in deep discussion when two members of the school council wandered over, shook hands and began questioning the two old-timers.

"Big tree, eh … Ever cut down a tree this size?"

"Yeah," replied Mantis.

"Ever had any trouble?"

"Nah."

"Got enough equipment. Saws and ropes and stuff?"

"Yeah."

"How long will it take?"

"Depends how we do it."

"What do you mean? How do you think you'll do it?"

"Dunno yet."

"What options do you have?"

"Cut it down. Might blow it. Probably blow it."

"What do you mean blow it?"

"Cut a hole in the base and put a charge in it. Blow it up. Quicker than a saw."

"Isn't that dangerous?"

"Not if you know what you're doing."

"What does the charge do?"

"Just weakens the base and then we pull it over with our old truck."

"How?"

"With a chain."

"Not too sure about this. Something could go wrong."

"Safe. No worries."

"What if something goes wrong?"

"Nothin'll go wrong."

"Have you done it before?"

"Yeah."

"Where?"

"In the bush."

"Hope you know what you're doing."

"Yeah, we do."

"When can you do the job?"

"Next Wednesday."

"But that's a school day!"

"Kids can watch."

"Don't know about that."

"They'll be right. Might learn something."

With that, the two studied the huge tree once again before trudging off to their old truck and taking off down the road.

Wednesday arrived. The word had got around that the big gum tree was to be removed that morning. It wasn't every day that something as exciting as that happened during school hours. All the school kids were excited at being able to watch as the big tree crashed to the ground. The noise it would make, the dust it would raise! A lot of parents who were not at work decided to attend the spectacle. In fact, the mother's club had anticipated the interest and were selling cakes, biscuits and other produce they had made from tables set up on the gravel oval down towards the pine trees.

Mantis and Sticka arrived in their old truck and drove in the back gate and down to where they were to operate on the gum tree. They jumped out and waved to some of the parents who were clapping them. Sticka even bowed. They got to work taking saws and axes and a brown wooden box off the tray of the truck. They placed the box carefully on the ground and once again studied the tree. Mantis pointed in a particular direction and Sticka nodded. Apparently, that was where they hoped the tree would fall when they pulled it over with the truck, after the charge weakened the base.

By now myself, Leany and Riddy and the rest of the kids were filing out of our classrooms and making a semi-circle on the oval close enough to the big tree so that we could see the two men preparing for the big event.

"Sir, what are they doing?"

"Stepping out the distance to where the tree should fall when they pull it over."

"Sir, how are they going to blow it up?"

"They're not blowing it up. They will use an explosive to weaken the base of the tree and then pull it over."

"What's the explosive called?"

"I don't know. Probably dynamite or gelignite."

"Will it be loud?"

"I don't think so …"

"Sir, how much do they use?"

"I don't know. Probably just a little bit to weaken the base of the tree."

Sticka fired up his chainsaw, revved it and began to cut into the tree base. A hole was made very quickly, which seemed to surprise the two woodsmen. They studied the hole and walked around the tree. Mantis banged it with his metal bar and spoke to Sticka for quite some time. Mantis nodded and walked over to the wooden box. He very carefully took some bundles of something wrapped in shiny brown paper from it and took them over to the base of the tree. The two men knelt on the ground and very, very carefully unwrapped what appeared to be sticks of something and tied them together with tape.

Hundreds of eyes followed every movement.

"Sir, what are they doing?"

"Putting the explosives in the base of the tree."

"Why?"

"I've already told you."

"It was a big bundle, sir."

"They know what they are doing."

The crowd continued to grow. Neighbours from around the school joined the anticipating crowd. Half the small oval was covered with grown-ups and students. And as people always do in a crowd, they slowly pressed forward in an effort to get closer to the action.

The mob hushed as Mantis and Sticka once again approached the tree. Sticka had moved the old truck to where it was needed when the time came to pull over the tree. As they did regularly, they discussed the situation. They looked into the hole where the charge was and craned their necks to peer up to the top of the monstrous tree. Sticka shook his head and appeared hesitant. He pointed to the base and motioned all the way to the top where a few hollow limbs could be seen. But Mantis just shook his head and again knelt beside the tree. Sticka walked quickly to shelter behind a pine tree. Mantis pulled out a box of matches from his pocket and struck one.

"Sir, what's he doing?"

"Lighting the fuse."

"What's the fuse?"

"The piece of string."

"Why?"

"You'll soon find out!"

Mantis put the match to the fuse, made sure it was spluttering and took off behind the pine trees.

Silence.

Not a sound.

You could have heard a fairy fart, as Dad would say!

Time stood still.

A wisp of smoke wafted from the hole in the tree.

Suddenly, an almighty boom shook the whole town. The whole tree rose from the ground and exploded into a million pieces. Sticks and leaves and bits of wood and bark and a number of demented possums rained down not just over the entire school but over the surrounding houses and roads. People and kids thought the end of the world had come. Covered in the remnants of the tree, they raced around in shock, screaming and tripping over each other in their haste to escape the carnage.

A dust cloud covered the school and neighbourhood. Many people still had their hands over their ears. The mother's club stall was ruined. Cakes and biscuits had disappeared under a layer of tree bits. The deafened possums, unhurt by their flight and landing, scrambled about among the rabble, no doubt wondering what the hell had happened.

From behind the pine trees, Mantis yelled, "We did it. The tree's gone!"

Sticka was in a state of shock. He stood there muttering to himself with his hands still over his ears. "God almighty …" he muttered. They both looked at where the tree had been. The only thing left was a large crater half full of debris and a few tufts of grey fur. Most of the pine trees had lost a lot of their foliage.

"We might have used a stick or two more than we needed, Sticka," Mantis remarked.

"I told you the whole tree was rotten and hollow!" replied Sticka. "But you wouldn't listen."

"Well, we don't have to pull it over now, Sticka."

"But look at the mess. I hope we don't have to clean it up," groaned Sticka.

"No, that wasn't in the contract. All we had to do was to remove the tree and the roots and we did that."

"Did we ever," added Sticka. "I hope they still pay us."

By now the crowd had dispersed. No one appeared badly injured. A few had cuts and abrasions, while a few were still suffering from some hearing problems. But all would recover in time. Some were standing in small groups, even laughing and gesturing and pointing to where the tree had once stood. The kids, after a good brush down, were back in class, no doubt discussing with their teachers what had just happened and why the tree disintegrated. Some traumatised youngsters were allowed to go home with their parents if they were able to. But most of the kids looked upon the experience as something special. Something to remember for a long time. The day the tree blew up!

The fire brigade arrived, annoyed at the absence of a fire, and swiftly returned to their base. Lots of rumours swept the town as to the cause of the explosion, but all was explained with a photo of the crater in the local newspaper the next day.

It took weeks for the mess to be cleaned up. The school council, parents, teachers and students spent days raking up the remains of the tree and removing it to the rubbish tip.

Mantis and Sticka laid low for a few months until they saw an advertisement in the paper for a tree removal and applied for the job. Dad said they didn't get it.

Collingwood

Dad called the stray cat Collingwood because it was black and white, had only one eye and appeared to be rather dense.

"Like most Collingwood football club supporters," he would say, grinning.

The mangy animal became a real nuisance. It skulked around the yard scrounging and stealing scraps and frightening the daylights out of the chooks and canaries. When disturbed it sprang in fright from unusual hiding places like Mum's washing basket or Dad's ferret-net bag. It sometimes made terrible noises on the roof at night. It even managed to squeeze into the ceiling of our house one day. When Dad saw and smelt something dripping onto his wireless, he swore that the mongrel cat had to go.

"No cats weein' on my wireless," he roared.

But catching the cat was easier said than done. Weeks of unsuccessful attempts to trap the pitiful creature passed; Collingwood was still at large and tormenting the life out of us. Dad was becoming unbearable.

Christmas Day was fast approaching and that year we were having a real treat for our Christmas dinner.

"It's a surprise," Dad said one day in early November as he arrived home with a huge lump in an old hessian bag. We followed him down the backyard and gazed in amazement as the bag was undone and the contents carefully tipped on the ground.

"It's a turkey," I cried. "What a whopper." The turkey blinked in the sunlight for a moment, stretched its legs and strutted around the yard. "Wow, look at its drumsticks. I bag one on Christmas Day," I added excitedly.

We watched while Dad went into the shed and returned with a handful of wheat. He threw it on the ground near the turkey and smiled as it gobbled it down.

"We'll give it lots of wheat and bread," said Dad. "Really fatten it up for Christmas."

Bonfire night was one of the highlights of the year and

preparations began many weeks before the big event. Branches, dry grass, old tyres and other burnable rubbish had to be collected and heaped in a clearing in the backyard or the nearest vacant block. Sometimes groups of families would work together and the result would be a huge bonfire that burnt for many hours.

Crackers and fireworks of all descriptions could be bought freely at most shops and, of course, the more money you had, the more crackers you could buy. Every penny earned or scrounged was saved in an effort to buy the best available.

Leany had struck it rich. His uncle had given him a job for a few weeks feeding pigs on Saturday mornings. He had saved his money until he had over two pounds tucked away in his Kool Mint tin.

"I'm gonna spend the flippin' lot on crackers," he announced. "Got m'eye on one of those whoppin' skyrockets. You know the big red and blue one in the flippin' window over at Hooper's shop. Costs five shillings, but I reckon it's worth it. Pickles Pickford had one of them," went on Leany. "So big he could hardly carry it. Had to stand it up in one of them concrete pot plants to light it. Should have heard it take off. Scared the hell out of Pickles. Went for miles too. Landed near Mr Tilley's old draught horse. Boy, did he go. Would've won the Melbourne Cup."

That afternoon we rode our bikes over to Hooper's shop to admire the huge rocket in the window.

"Strewth." Riddy chuckled. "Sure looks powerful. I reckon we could all sit on it and get a free ride."

"Hey, we could tie stuff on it like streamers and balloons," I suggested.

"How about a parachute, Spike? Do ya reckon it would work?" added Leany. "We could watch it float down."

"Don't be stupid," interrupted Riddy. "It'll be nighttime. How ya gonna see it?"

"Set it off during the day," I answered. "Doesn't matter about coloured lights and things that shoot out. Still see 'em anyway. Just not as bright."

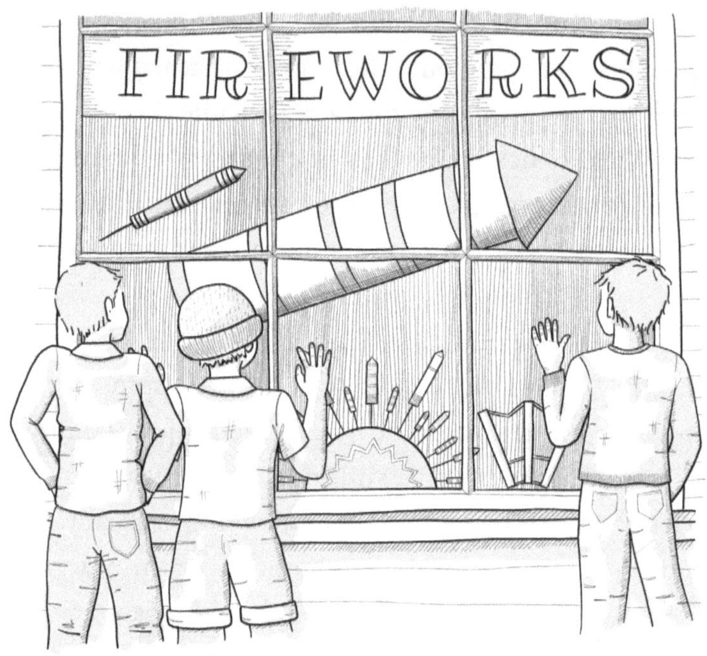

"I'll get the rocket in the morning. You two can get the flippin' streamers and balloons and make the parachute," said Leany excitedly, his face flushing as he thought about it.

Next morning, Leany arrived with the rocket wrapped up in an enormous piece of brown cardboard. We already had the streamers and balloons ready to attach to it.

The parachute was a little more difficult to prepare. We found a picture of one in a magazine and tried to copy the diagram. We needed a large piece of material and found one of

Mum's old dresses in the washhouse. The fact that it was bright red with white spots didn't deter us.

"Easier to see," said Riddy.

We cut out a large circle about the size of a washing basket and tied pieces of string to it at various places around the edge. We then joined these together about a yard from the material. It looked good.

"We'd better try it out," suggested Riddy. "Tie a piece of wood onto it and chuck it in the air."

The experiment appeared to work surprisingly well. The wood floated to the ground.

"No worries," I cried. "Now for the real thing."

We tied the streamers and balloons to the stick of the rocket. The parachute was last to be attached at the bottom. We stood admiring our handiwork.

Riddy and I rolled out a large iron drum from inside one of the sheds and stood it upright in the middle of the backyard. Leany carried the rocket over and stood it inside. He then arranged the decorations inside the drum away from the wick and decided that because of its length the parachute would be best folded and put on the ground beside the drum.

Because it was Leany's rocket, it was decided that he would be the one to launch it. He would put the match to the wick and then run like mad to the woodheap from where we were able to watch the incredible event.

"Okay, give her the works," roared Riddy, crouching down behind the wood.

Leany very gingerly struck a match and stretched it towards the rocket. He placed it against the wick and sprinted towards us. He was scrambling up the woodheap when suddenly there was a crash at the middle gate and we heard the shrill yelping of our fox terrier. A black and white cat flew over the fence.

"It's Collingwood!"

"The dog's chasin''im."

The cat hurtled across the clearing, searching frantically for somewhere to hide. The dust flew as it skidded to a halt and shot into the heap of red and white material beside the drum.

"Hell, it's hiding in the flippin' parachute," screamed Leany, waving his arms. He picked up a large chip of wood and hurled it at the mound of material. "Get outta there, ya mongrel," he roared. "Scram. It's goin' up any second. You'll spoil it."

The spluttering of the wick suddenly turned into a roar and the balloons and streamers in the drum bounced and fluttered. There was a flash of light and the huge rocket rose in a flurry of sparks and smoke. But almost immediately, the rocket's departure was anchored by the added weight of Collingwood inside the parachute.

The rocket strained to lift the load off the ground. It rose ever so slowly to the level of the shed roof, the streamers, balloons and the bulging parachute all dangling from the stick.

An ear-splitting bang rang through the air and three bright blue stars shot from the rocket. The explosion and the flash of light must have frightened the whiskers off Collingwood because he was jolted into frantic action. He began tearing and reefing in a frenzied bid to escape from the swaying parachute. This had an unfortunate effect on the labouring rocket. As the cat screeched and struggled, the nose of the huge missile dropped until it lay parallel to the ground and with a mighty roar took off across the yard with its load in tow.

We watched as Collingwood poked his head from within the folds of the material, his one eye almost popping out of its socket in terror. Each time the cat scrambled about, the rocket changed direction so that its path was zigzagged and unpredictable.

Unfortunately, Dad's big turkey decided it was time for a feed and was strutting past the water dish when he was crunched on the head by the now speeding rocket. The turkey dropped like a stone and, apart from a few final twitches, lay motionless.

"God, it's killed him," yelled Leany. "Dead as a maggot."

The rocket appeared to have a new lease of life and, having glanced off the turkey's head, shot over the chook shed, over the corrugated iron fence and into the next-door neighbour's yard. The terrified cat didn't appreciate being bounced across the chook shed roof and continued his howling and tearing at an even greater rate in an endeavour to escape.

Old Mrs Singleton was busy pegging out the washing on the clothesline. She was standing legs apart, bending over her washing basket, when, with a roar, the rocket dipped and hit the ground between her feet. She screamed and despite her old age sprang amazingly high into the air. The three red stars that thundered from the rocket at the same instant did little to help the situation. One of them landed in the hem of her long apron and she lit up like a Roman candle. She fled up the path, leaving a trail of pegs and smoke.

The rocket continued. It snaked across the vegetable garden, deflected off a cabbage and headed for the old ramshackle toilet in the corner of the yard. It was a pity old Mr Singleton had to be sitting in there at that very moment. The rocket smashed into the wall, crunched through the rotted boards and came to an abrupt stop inches from the old boy's head. The noise of the spluttering rocket and the hysterical howling of the cat filled the little building. He burst out and followed his wife up the path, clutching at his pants hanging down around his knees.

The doctor said later that the old couple would recover in time from their terrible ordeal, but we didn't see them for ages.

Collingwood eventually escaped from the parachute and was last seen hurtling over the railway line. Dad would be pretty pleased that the cat had disappeared. But he wouldn't be too happy about having to pay for the Singletons' new toilet. The sparks from the rocket had ignited the old boards, and in the twinkling of an eye, all that was left was a steaming toilet pan sizzling on the brick floor.

And that wasn't all the strife I was in. We stared fearfully at what was left of the turkey – a lifeless, feathered bundle sprawled out in the dust of the chook yard.

"Perhaps you can still eat it," said Leany as we stood over the corpse. The dull drone of several blowflies made us think twice about this plan.

"Have to scrape the maggots off first." Riddy grinned, forgetting, for a moment, the seriousness of the situation.

"I don't want Dad to know we've killed it," I said. "He'll murder me. Or worse still, he might keep me indoors on bonfire night."

We had big plans for bonnie night, plans we didn't want ruined by a dead gobbler.

Then Leany had a brainwave.

"Why not build the bonnie now and hide the flippin' turkey under the branches."

"Yeah," I agreed. "Sort of like one of them cremations. Nothin' left but ashes."

We set to work immediately, heaping the dead branches we had collected in a pile in the middle of the yard. The turkey was tucked away in the centre of the funeral pyre, hidden by the branches and dead grass.

We finished the bonnie – despite its rushed construction, it looked pretty good.

"There, now we can relax." Riddy sighed as he slumped to the ground. "And forget about the turkey. Ya dad won't find it now."

I was still a bit worried though.

"What if it starts to stink?" I asked. "He might smell it. He's down here cutting wood and feedin' the ferrets and collectin' the eggs all the time."

"Well, you spend a lot of flippin' time here too. If you notice any stink, we'll have to get it out and seal it in a bag or something," snapped Leany. "It'll only be there for two days anyway. Stop worryin', will ya?"

By Saturday morning I was feeling much better. The bonfire would be lit that night, we would let our crackers off and there would be no trace left of the dead turkey.

Mind you, Dad didn't take long to notice that our Christmas dinner had disappeared.

"Some mongrel's stolen it," he roared, squinting into the distance as if he'd be able to see them running away with the turkey.

"Yeah, I bet that's what's happened," I said, agreeing with him. "I wonder who took it?"

Dad stormed off to cut some wood. I followed him down the path, through the gate and into the backyard. I sniffed the air nervously when I passed the hidden turkey, but all I could smell was the gum leaves and dead grass of the bonfire.

I wandered over to where Dad was splitting the wood. As he furiously cut, I stacked the wheelbarrow.

Suddenly, I was distracted by a rustling behind me and glanced over to the bonnie. I couldn't believe my eyes. I looked at Dad. He had stopped chopping and was staring at something moving in the leaves, the axe still poised over his shoulder.

We watched, scarcely daring to breathe, as a black and white tail appeared from the branches. The black tip twitched from side to side. Then a back leg struggled out and planted itself firmly on the ground. Another leg felt its way through the leaves and a little cloud of dust rose as it struggled for a foothold. The two legs yanked and strained and gradually a body slowly appeared.

"It's that mongrel cat," whispered Dad. "What the hell's he doin'?"

Collingwood's head popped out from the leaves. So focused on what was in front him was he that he didn't realise he was being watched.

He continued his tugging and heaving and to my horror I suddenly realised what he was up to. The colour drained from my face. I glanced at Dad.

"What's he got hangin' out of his mouth?" he mumbled. "Looks like a chook's head."

As we watched, the neck and upper body of the "chook" was dragged in jerks from the bonnie. The cat struggled to move the huge carcass. Dad's expression morphed from one of curiosity to one of anger. I can't really write what he roared at the cat. He usually didn't swear much, but when he saw the dead gobbler being dragged from the branches by the one-eyed cat, he exploded.

"The 'so-and-so's killed our 'so-and-so' turkey," he bellowed and, with the axe still raised above his head, charged at the surprised cat. Collingwood, now in a state of utter confusion, dropped the turkey's head and jumped sideways into the air, his one eye glued on the glinting axe. Not wishing to be chopped to pieces, he shot back into the branches of the bonnie.

"I'll fix the blighter," snarled Dad, whipping a box of matches from his pocket.

"No, Dad!" I cried. "No. Don't light it now. It's for tonight. You'll ruin it for tonight."

But it was too late. The dead leaves were crackling and a wisp of smoke rose into the air.

"Quick, get around the other side. Make sure he doesn't escape," Dad yelled. "If he sticks his head out, whack him with that rake there."

I grabbed the rake and stood watching the burning pile of rubbish. Riddy and Leany wouldn't be too happy about this at all. Suddenly, a black and white blur burst from the smoke and flames, shot between my legs and disappeared into the woodshed. I swung the rake but didn't get within a bull's roar of hitting the speeding cat.

"See 'im yet?" yelled Dad above the noise of the fire.

I swallowed hard and looked back at the woodshed. "No. No. Not yet. Must be dead by now."

"Yeah, we've barbequed him. Got rid of the mongrel at last," gloated Dad. "Thank God he's gone."

I rejoined Dad on the other side of the smouldering remains of the bonfire.

"Give me the rake," he said.

He put the rake under the singed carcass of the turkey and with a groan heaved the remains into the middle of the coals.

"Didn't really think a cat would kill a turkey that size," he pondered. "But I s'pose if they're hungry enough … Sorry about the bonfire. Anyway, come and give me a hand to feed those roosters. They'll have to be fattened up for Christmas."

Four on the Floor

"Not another plant," grumped Dad. "Haven't we got enough now? What is it anyway?"

"It's an ornamental chilli," answered Mum. "I've never seen one before. It's pretty, isn't it?"

I glanced up from the *Phantom* comic I was reading. I was quite impressed, for a change, with Mum's choice of plants. This one was different. About a foot high, shiny leaves and about twenty red and yellow cone-shaped things sticking up from the branches like Christmas tree decorations.

"Stick it out on the back verandah," said Dad. "It stinks."

Mum sniffed at the plant delicately. "Yes, it does a bit. I suppose a bit of sun won't do it any harm. Will you take it out please, dear?"

I threw down the comic, picked up the plant and unceremoniously carted it out and plonked it by the backdoor.

Honk, our fox terrier, was sprawled out near the bottom step enjoying the warmth of the sun. He appeared to be asleep but occasionally would lift his head and snap at the flies buzzing around his nose. I sat down on the step beside him. The red and yellow cones of the new plant glinted in the sun. I reached out and snapped one off its branch. I held it between my fingers and gently squeezed it. It was quite hard, but after some heavy squeezing, it popped and split open, revealing a number of small, flat, round seeds about the size of a ladybug. I carefully pulled one from the pod and examined it. The seed was covered in a sticky substance and when I tried to drop it on the floor it stuck to my finger. I finally removed it by flicking it off with my other hand. I watched it land inches from Honk's head. Immediately, an eye partly opened, a pink tongue shot out and the seed disappeared.

I was about to relax in the warmth of the sun again when the dog shot to his feet and let out an almighty yelp. He took off round the house, shaking his head. Coming to an abrupt stop, he pawed at his mouth with his front feet, whimpering and whining. I watched in astonishment as he raced back onto the verandah, hurtled three times round the rocking chair and headed for his tin of water under the lemon tree. I didn't think a dog Honk's size could drink so much water, but finally he lifted his head and flopped down on the dirt, panting.

I took another seed, placed it on my finger and very cautiously put it on the tip of my tongue. For a few seconds, I felt nothing. A terrible burning sensation crept up the back of my throat, making me gasp for air, and I spat out the seed and rushed to the tap. Later, when the stinging had stopped and I examined my tongue in a mirror, I found a small white blister had developed where the seed had been.

Mum played the piano at the local church and was a hard-working member of the Church Guild – a collection of well-meaning but gasbagging women who met in the Sunday School Hall once a month to exchange recipes and gossip. The Guild Committee met a few days before these meetings at members' homes around the town. Today was Mum's turn to host the committee meeting. Today was also the last Friday of the September school holidays. My friend Riddy and I were melting lead under the peppercorn tree in the backyard. I was pouring the lead into a mould when the side gate rattled.

"Old Bert, the minister," I said, scarcely looking up from my job.

Old Bert had been the local minister for many, many years. He rode an old brown bicycle and always wore a pair of silver bicycle clips to stop his black pants from getting caught in the chain. He was a tiny bloke with a sandy complexion and weather-beaten face. But the main feature of his nut-like head was a huge set of buck teeth that protruded at an unfortunate angle from between his lips. They were so big and stuck out so far that he could never close his mouth properly. Dad said that Old Bert had been known to eat an apple through a tennis racquet.

Bert was followed at intervals by the other members of the committee, a varied collection of archaics all dressed in hats and coats. Each had a plate of sandwiches or cakes for the afternoon tea.

"Aw, hell no." Riddy sighed. "Look who's here."

Mrs Nicholson had brought little Harry with her. He trotted beside Mrs Nicholson, carrying a jar of water with two brown teeth bobbing around inside. He was a pale-skinned little twit with a head resembling an albino ferret. Riddy didn't like little Harry very much at all and spent a lot of his time planning tricks to play on him in an endeavour to upset the youngster.

Like last month when Mrs Nicholson and Harry visited Mum, who was in bed with a bad cold. Riddy and I found an old nest of bantam eggs in the wood heap. They had obviously been there for many months and rattled ominously when they were shaken. I had heard somewhere that when you put an egg lengthways between your two hands it can't be broken, no matter how hard you squeeze. We were testing the theory out when little Harry stuck his head over the middle fence to see what we were doing.

"G'day, ferret face," said Riddy. "Let ya out of ya cage, did they?"

Little Harry ignored the comment and watched as we continued to squeeze the eggs.

"Want a go, Harry?" invited Riddy. "They won't break."

He demonstrated the procedure, his face straining in his attempt to break the egg while Harry looked on in amazement.

"Here, have this egg. Come on. Have a go. It won't break."

Harry sidled through the gate and took the egg. Riddy

positioned the egg lengthways between Harry's hands and beckoned him to squeeze. Harry cautiously applied a little pressure and when nothing happened, called on full strength. The egg remained intact.

"Now put it the other way," Riddy went on. "It's even stronger that way."

Harry turned the egg sideways and again mustered full strength, his face twisted as if in pain.

A loud pop sounded, like a balloon bursting, and the egg exploded a foot from Harry's face. A green-greyish liquid erupted from within and splattered over the entire front of the unfortunate victim. Harry didn't know what hit him. The stink was unbearable. Little Harry let out a wail, turned and, with the putrid egg dripping from his face, hands and clothes, fled up the path to his mother. Riddy and I hadn't seen anything so hilarious for a long time, but Mrs Nicholson was not at all amused. They cut the visit short and went home. Harry spent a long time in the bath and his stinking clothes were thrown in the rubbish bin.

It was no wonder we didn't see Harry's head appear over the fence today. In fact, he didn't dare leave his mother's side at all.

The one good thing about these meetings was the afternoon tea. As soon as we thought we could hear the cups and saucers rattling, we would appear as if by magic and join in the feast.

We were just heading in the door when Riddy noticed Mum's new plant with its cones shining in the sun.

"What's that?"

"Mum's chilli."

"What are those things on it?"

"Seed pods. But don't touch them, they'll burn ya tongue off."

"Give me a look at one." Riddy grabbed a red cone and gingerly rolled it around in his fingers.

"The seeds are inside," I said.

Using his fingernail, Riddy split the skin and stared at the little white seeds.

"Can't be too hot. They're not very big."

"Yeah, you try one," I answered.

He touched a seed with his finger and licked it cautiously. He stared at me for a few seconds, fear filling his eyes, before dashing for the tap.

"Hell," he spluttered as he swirled the cold water around his mouth. "Burn the bum off a lizard." He picked up the seed pod he'd dropped on the verandah floor and again studied it intently. "They look like tomato seeds, don't they?" he said slowly. "Ya wouldn't know the difference." His voice was soft as if he was talking to himself.

I could almost see his brain ticking over under his green hat.

"I wonder if Harry likes tomato sandwiches?"

We looked at each other and grinned. Riddy carefully wrapped the red cone in his hanky and we crept into the kitchen. Mum was pouring tea. Plates of cakes and sandwiches were on the kitchen table.

"Oh, there you are, you two. I thought it was about time you arrived. Perhaps you can help me now that you're here. You can bring in the food and put it on the dining room table."

She headed off carrying a tray of steaming cups of tea.

"Quick," Riddy whispered. "Open up one of those tomato sandwiches. I'll whack some seeds in it and we'll give it to ferret head."

The sandwich was quickly doctored and placed at the end

of the row beside Riddy's hand. I picked up a plate of cream puffs and together we marched into the dining room.

The archaics were sitting around the room chatting. Little Harry was sitting on the floor beside his mother's chair looking terribly bored.

"Here, have a tomato sandwich," said Riddy, shoving the plate under Harry's pale face. "This one here looks a good 'un. You like tomato sandwiches, don't you? Here have this one."

Harry's bony little hand crept out to take a sandwich.

"Don't you dare, Harold," snapped his mother. "You know what tomatoes do to you, dear." She leant over to Old Bert who was sitting next to her. "Gives him the runs, they do," she explained to the minister. "Can't eat 'em at all."

Old Bert glanced at the plate of sandwiches. "I'll have one, thank you," he said and quickly took the one offered to little Harry.

"No, not that one," squeaked Riddy. "I-I-I, er … dropped that one on the kitchen floor."

"Oh, it'll be fine. Take more than a bit of dirt to kill me." He cackled. He thrust the whole sandwich past his protruding teeth into his mouth.

Riddy and I looked at each other and then back to the minister who was by now chewing heartedly and listening to Mrs Nicholson's version of the bantam egg incident. They both looked in our direction, shaking their heads. Old Bert swallowed half his sandwich and continued to fervently chew the remainder.

Little Harry's prized possession, his two brown teeth in the jar of water, had been brought to the meeting for everyone to admire. The teeth had fallen out of his mouth during breakfast that morning and Harry had readied them for the fairies to collect that night. Now they were sitting in the jar on the mantelpiece.

All at once, Old Bert stopped chewing. He stared wide-eyed at Mrs Nicholson, sitting bolt upright as if hit on the head with a mallet. Mrs Nicholson looked at him strangely and was just about to ask if he was feeling unwell when the minister let out a strangled screech and flew from his chair. One hand covered his mouth and teeth and the other clutched his throat. The other members of the committee looked on in fright as Bert, in his haste to flee from the room, tripped over little Harry and crashed to the floor.

"Heart attack!" shrieked Mrs Nicholson. "He's dying."

"Keep him still. Hold him down," yelled Mrs Dunn.

"Watch he doesn't bite," warned Mrs Potter.

But Old Bert was already crawling towards the door, the remainder of the tomato sandwich spilling from his mouth onto the carpet. He croaked something about burning and water and, still clawing at his mouth and throat, struggled to his feet. Spying the jar of water on the mantelpiece, he gulped the lot down in the twinkling of an eye.

"My teeth!" wailed little Harry. "He's swallowed my teeth. Mum, get 'em back!"

Mrs Nicholson rushed over to Bert and thumped him on the back in an effort to retrieve Harry's teeth. Poor Old Bert was sent flying across the room and smashed headfirst into the fire grate. Luckily the fire was not going, but when Bert reappeared, he looked different. His mouth was closed and four huge teeth were scattered on the tiled hearth.

Bert forgot about his burning mouth and throat for a moment. He stared at the teeth lying forlorn before him and, as if he didn't believe his eyes, felt the space where they had once been.

"My teef," he hissed. "My teef."

Little Harry summed up the situation in a glance. His teeth were gone but he was certainly not missing out on the fairies.

"I'll swap ya," he cried, swooping on the four on the floor. "I'll have yours."

But Bert didn't hear. It was all too much for him, and as Mrs Dunn fell to her knees to pray, he sank slowly to the floor and fainted.

The ambulance man didn't take long to arrive and before long Bert was on his way to hospital. He looked quite miserable with a wad of cotton wool sticking from his mouth and a wet cloth draped over his throat. Meanwhile Harry had refilled his jar with water and had dropped the four teeth in.

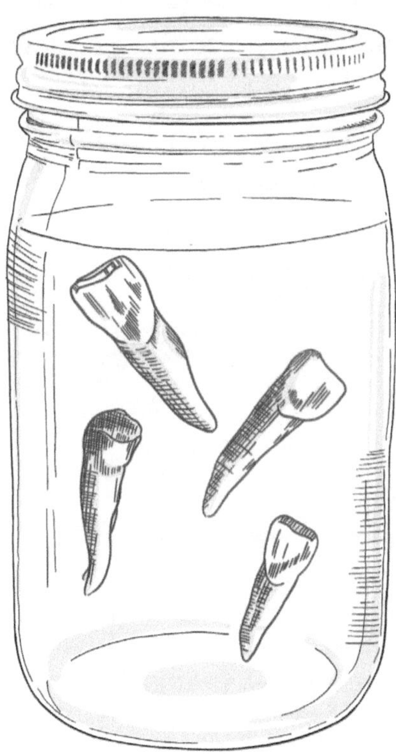

I don't know if he doubled his money or not when the fairies took the teeth. But I bet they got a shock when they saw Harry's little head on the pillow and the enormous teeth in the jar.

After a short holiday, Old Bert resumed his duties at the church, sporting a shiny set of false teeth, which certainly improved his appearance a great deal.

Apart from the dentures, he didn't seem to have suffered any permanent ill effects from his dose of hot chilli seeds.

He often referred to the incident as an act of God.

"God works in mysterious ways," he would say, flashing his new teeth.

Riddy and I didn't do much wrong for the next couple of weeks. We surprised everyone with our helpfulness and thoughtful behaviour. We weren't sure if my parents suspected we were to blame or not. That was until Dad came in one morning with something small stuck on his fingers.

"These chilli seeds look a bit like tomato seeds, don't they?" he mumbled, looking directly at me. He then grabbed a large glass, filled it with water and gulped it down.

"Pretty hot too," he rasped, still glaring menacingly at me.

Through Coloured Windows

In those days, I didn't think in depth about people dying. Us kids had more important things to worry about, like how to get out of folk dancing at school or where to go fishing at the weekend. Most of us went to Sunday school and church, which sort of spoilt each Sunday morning. I had to get spruced up in my grey suit and shiny shoes and act as if the whole charade was doing me and my inner self the world of good. Sitting in church was probably the closest I ever got to thinking about death. People there appeared morbid and nodded silently to each other and crept around as if the devil himself was hiding behind the organ. Apart from a few nervous whispers and an occasional stifled cough, the only voice heard was that of the minister trying to convince the congregation that if they believed in God, they would be saved. I could never work out what the danger was. Apart from Sunday mornings, life was pretty good. I was having a great time; I didn't need saving. After the service, the minister would stand at the door and shake hands with everyone as if congratulating them on their endurance in sitting in the stark building instead of enjoying themselves elsewhere.

I never related God with a man-made building. Surely he would rather live out in the bush with the animals and the trees and the warm sun and welcome rain. In any case, he made all these things, and I could imagine him floating around admiring his handiwork and saying to himself, "Hell, I did a pretty good job, didn't I?"

Even though the church was supposed to be his house, I bet he only went there on a Sunday too. Of course, I couldn't see him in the church, but I knew where he was. He would have only liked two things in the church: the pretty-coloured windows and the vases of flowers that sat on a little side table in front of the pulpit. When the sun was shining through the windows, rays of coloured light reflected and danced on the floor, intermingling with the colours of the flowers. That's where he would be each Sunday, beside the flowers in the rainbow colours. He could just float there in his white robes and poke faces at the people he didn't like. I wished I could be there with him instead of sitting in the gloom on a cold, hard pew. I also knew he would be first out the door when the service had finished. He was lucky because no one was able to see him. He could rush out without shaking hands with the minister. He didn't have to stand around and gossip about who was sick or who was dying or who hadn't been seen at church for a while. I usually spent this time looking for birds' nests in the cypress trees that surrounded the churchyard or trying to catch the little geckos that lay sunbaking on the rocks. I knew God was back out in the bush by the time we headed for home.

Occasionally my friend Riddy came with us to church. Mum would make a point of asking him on a Saturday if he was doing anything on the following Sunday morning. If he wasn't quick enough with an answer, we would pick him up on the way. Mum liked to take Riddy under her wing when she could. He lived with his father in a rather old but neat house with a green roof and a huge front verandah. His mother had died many years previously, and because Riddy's father worked long hours, he was left to fend for himself much of the time. During school holidays, he would have many of his meals with us and on occasion stay the night. We accepted each other's company without question. In a sense, he had become part of our family and usually accompanied us on any outings or functions that we decided to attend.

Together with Leany, the two of us spent most of our spare time in the bush. Nearly every holiday, weekend and afternoon after school we could be found bird nesting, rabbiting, fishing or collecting bottles along the roads. We shared secrets, stories and jokes. Over the years, we developed a strong affinity with the bush. We knew where the mushrooms and wildflowers grew, in which trees and shrubs particular birds would nest, the colours of their eggs, the ways and habits of the bush animals, snakes, lizards and insects. We learnt how and where to fish and how to read and predict the weather. Each day was different, something new to discover, to touch, to smell, to inspect and to marvel at. Here was our place of worship. We were as one with nature and I still recall this time vividly and remain to this day in awe of the bush and all its mystique and beauty.

"Let's go bird nesting," suggested Riddy one day after school as the two of us sat on the rocking chairs near our back door.

"Where? We haven't got time to go far."

"What about the trottin' track? Haven't been there for a while. Might be some maggies nesting in the cypress trees."

Because the trotting track wasn't far from our house, we decided to jog over rather than ride our bikes. Besides, we had to cross the step-bridge over the railway lines and it was no fun dragging bikes up and over that. The trotting track was a favourite haunt for the neighbourhood kids. There were plenty of trees to climb, sand hills to jump from and small dams where we could go yabbying and tadpoling.

We entered the track through a well-used hole in the corrugated iron fence and walked to the clump of trees growing behind the old grandstand. A brick toilet was situated between the grandstand and the back fence. This area was dominated by a number of huge cypress and peppercorn trees. It was a simple matter to scale to the top of the toilet roof and onto the branches of the thick trees. They grew so very close to each other that we could pass from tree to tree without ever touching the ground. We were soon picking across and up the branches, Riddy leading the way in the search for a nest. We climbed higher and higher towards the top of the thick trees, the wind sighing through the leaves and the sun trying to reach the shadows around us.

The muffled sound came upon us from nowhere and I hugged the branch I was on for dear life. I slowly opened my eyes and looked to where Riddy was a moment ago. He wasn't there. The leaves and branches near where he had been were black and smoke filled the surrounding area. I looked down and saw Riddy lying on his back across the lower branches where he had been thrown by the explosion. Smoke too was coming from his green hat and his smouldering shoes. I yelled and yelled at him, but he didn't answer. He didn't move. I half climbed, half fell down the tree and ran for help.

I never saw him again. Electricity had smashed through his body when his head touched the power line and blew holes in his head and his feet.

There was not a lot of people in the church. Family friends and a few classmates made up the numbers. It was Wednesday and everyone sat in silence, looking straight ahead. Mum was crying. Even though it wasn't Sunday, I knew God was there in his usual spot beside the flowers in the coloured lights. Riddy would be there too, floating with him in the dancing colours, talking and pointing and smiling. Riddy would have been one of God's special friends. They both loved the bush, and God would have watched us and followed us through the trees and over the creeks and around the rocks. He would have known us very well. The two of them would leave together before everyone else. I knew where they were going.

I ran home. I cried all the way. I jumped on my bike and rode and rode through the bush tracks as fast as I could until

I could ride no further. I ran, exhausted, through the trees and jumped the creeks and logs. I kicked the rocks and hurled sticks and sobbed and cried. I yelled at the birds and challenged the bees to bite me. Finally, I dropped to the ground, curled up in a ball and lay panting on the grass. At ground level I could see the ants scurrying along well-used tracks, their little black bodies glistening in the sunlight. Grains of sand shone and rippled with colour. The gum leaves reflected the sun's rays and the birds sang and the insects buzzed and whirred. Light illuminated the whole area. Colours danced and flitted and vibrated. I knew that Riddy was where he loved to be. He and God would look after each other and care for all the animals and plants that lived around them. I knew too that I could always talk to Riddy on my many visits to the bush and look to where he and God floated near the flowers in the church.

But I was not the same for a long time.

The Rats Steal the Show

Friday night was picture night for most of the kids in town. The "flicks" were held in the town hall on Wednesday, Friday and Saturday nights. But Friday night was the kids' special night. It didn't matter what films were being shown, we would still be there. You could tell by the noise level during the film whether it was good or not. Westerns and horror movies were the favourites, while musicals and love stories were not appreciated. As the interest decreased during such films, the noise level would rise accordingly.

In those days, going to the flicks meant staying for two films separated by an intermission known as half-time. We also watched news reels and cartoons. All this generally took about four hours and, because television did not exist then, the picture nights were well patronised and (apart from the musicals and love stories) very entertaining.

Half-time was when most kids raced out and bought their refreshments. There was a kiosk in the hall where you could buy lollies and drinks, but most kids favoured running to the two shops over the road where you could buy hot food such as fish and chips or pies and hamburgers. I always joined the mad race over there and always bought a shilling worth of fish and chips.

The only problem was hot food was not supposed to be taken into the town hall and this was reinforced by a large sign on the screen at half-time that said:

DO NOT BRING TAKEAWAY FOOD INTO THIS HALL
IT WILL ATTRACT RATS

Of course, this didn't deter us from smuggling in our hot food, hidden under coats and jumpers. The smell of all this gave the game away but no one seemed to police the rules and so it was open slather!

But this was to suddenly change …

Nearly all the kids were seated upstairs on the balcony and usually in the same seats, week after week. The balcony hovered above half of the ground floor seats and had a safety wall of about three or four feet high – they didn't want anyone toppling over the edge. This didn't stop the usual idiots from flicking lollies or other bits and pieces down onto the people sitting below.

This particular Friday night was typical of any other Friday night. Half-time came and everyone raced away to get their hot food, knowingly smiling at the rat sign when they returned for the second film. The show was actually very exciting and everyone was engrossed in the action when an ear-splitting scream from a girl in one of the seats near the front of the balcony ripped through the air.

"It's a rat!"

"There's a rat," echoed another voice.

"Argh, a rat!"

And sure enough, there *was* a huge rat. Not just one but two of them, creeping along the top of the balcony safety wall. All the kids near the rats, especially the girls, yelled and screamed and all hell broke loose.

Without thinking, some idiot who was sitting right near the rats threw his bottle of soft drink at the first one. It was a good throw but most unfortunately planned, as the bottle hit the rat and both sailed over the balcony wall, landing among the people sitting downstairs. Old Frank Hanger – people called him Coat – and his wife Myrtle were the unlucky couple who copped the brunt of the action. The bottle hit Coat on the top of his bald head and, groaning, he slid to the floor. The rat landed on Myrtle's lap and she yelled and screamed like a banshee. She swiped at it with her old, weathered hands. In a state of terror, the rat raced along the laps of all the people seated in that row. The panic and screams escalated and soon there was a stampede for the exits. A lot of the crowd had no idea what the emergency was, but they were not hanging around. They rushed to the doors.

Meanwhile, upstairs, the other rat had jumped to the floor and disappeared between the rows of seats until it attempted a death-defying stunt by running up Prue Curran's leg. Again, pandemonium reigned and there was a mass exodus, mainly screaming girls, for the doors. Some of the older boys saw the funny side of the whole episode and only worsened the situation by yelling, "Rat! Rats … more of 'em!". Nevertheless, they too decided not to stay and followed the hysterical mob from the hall.

Both the upstairs and downstairs crowd spilled out into the area at the front of the town hall. It wasn't long before the fire brigade arrived, followed by an ambulance and a police car, all unsure of what was going on. A growing number of concerned onlookers arrived as well, wondering what caused the mass flight from the hall.

In a few days the local newspaper reported the whole sorry story. The headlines read "Rats Steal the Show", and a detailed account of the incident together with eye-witness reports followed. A photo of Coat sitting up in a hospital bed with a big white bandage on his head accompanied the article.

The town hall council decided enough was enough. There would be no picture nights for two weeks while two rat catchers were employed to get rid of the rats. Dad said our fox terrier Harry would do a better job. When the pictures returned, two security guards were standing at the hall doors to ensure no one was smuggling in hot food. Some smart alecks could still cause some occasional panic by yelling out *"Rat!"* during pictures, but this soon died out when no one reacted. It was back to enjoying the flicks as long as it was not a musical or a love story.

But I missed my fish and chips.

Walter

Over the years, the rearing of and caring for a wide range of pets played an important role in the development of values and responsibilities of kids like me within many homes. As a youngster, the time spent with my dad and friends in the bush ensured I had a continual menagerie of animals and birds of all shapes and sizes. Dogs, cats, mice, rabbits, ferrets, lizards, tortoises, budgies, parrots, cockatoos, kookaburras, plovers, bantams and canaries all graced our home with their presence at some stage, and incidents involving some of these family members remain a talking point to this day.

One memorable event involved a mouse I called Walter. Walter was given to me by an older cousin whose original pair of mice had, in a short time, triggered a population explosion. One particular mouse became quite aggressive around his peers, and when he actually killed two of his family members, he was abruptly banished in disgrace to my house.

I grew very fond of Walter, and he became accustomed to travelling around with me, hidden in my pocket. Thankfully he showed no signs of his aggressive streak in his new home.

I was talking to a couple of kids at school one day and mentioned Walter had been given to me because he had killed two other mice. Word soon got round that I had a killer mouse that was the fiercest and most wildest in the whole district. I was quite proud of this and many times had to produce Walter from my pocket to allow groups of kids to peer in awe at the vicious killer.

Two boys I didn't like were Max and his mate Beetle. Truthfully, I was a bit scared of them. They were a pair of bullies and as such spent much of their time terrorising smaller kids who were continually tormented and threatened with all sorts of physical and mental abuse. They did all the things that bullies still do today. Unfortunately, they did a great deal to make life for their victims as difficult as they could.

Apparently, Max heard about Walter and one day made a point of cornering Leany and I on our way home from school.

"Where's ya mouse?" grunted Max.

"Home," I replied.

Max looked menacingly down at me. "Got any money on ya?"

I shook my head.

"Lost ya tongue, have ya, Spikey? Poke it out. Come on, give us a look at it." He looked at Beetle and winked. Beetle sniggered back at him. "Come on, Spikey boy. Give us a look."

I poked out my tongue.

"Did ya see that, Beetle? He poked out his tongue at us. I think we should give him a beltin' for doin' that."

I looked up at the two of them. Leany took a step back.

"Where do ya think you're goin'?" Max growled. "Ya not leavin' Spikey all on his own, are ya?"

I felt for sure that Leany and I would be going home with a blood nose each and a few bruises for good measure. But suddenly Max returned his thoughts to the whereabouts of Walter.

"So, ya mouse is at home, ya say," he drawled. "Ya got any money at home, Spikey?"

"No," I said softly.

"Aw, come on, Spikey boy, I bet ya have. Two bob?"

I looked at Max and wondered what he was getting at.

"I've got a mouse at home too, Spikey. I bet ya two bob he can beat yours in a fight."

I continued to look at him.

"What about it, Spikey boy? Your mouse against mine. I know ya will because if ya don't, I'll belt the livin' daylights out of ya."

Beetle laughed and thumped a clenched fist into his other open hand.

"Tomorrow. Four o'clock. Yard near the railway gates. Bring ya mouse. Ya know what will happen if ya don't."

Beetle again smashed his fist. Max took a step towards me and hissed between his teeth.

"See ya tomorrow, Spikey boy. Ya can stop shakin now," he added smugly.

He slowly drew his finger across his throat, looked at me for a moment then turned and strode off with Beetle.

The confrontation really shook me up. Even if Walter won the fight, I was sure I wouldn't get the two bob. I knew what I would get instead – I would cop a hiding. There would be other kids there to watch the battle, so I figured I was pretty safe until Max and Beetle caught up with me the next day. I would have to worry about that when the time came.

I was sure Walter could look after himself given his reputation, but I was still concerned about his welfare. I didn't want to see him get hurt. At four o'clock the next day, Leany and I arrived at the yard. I was pleased to see a dozen or so other kids standing around a large metal drum, which obviously was to be used as the boxing ring. Snake and Sniff, who I sometimes knocked around with, were among the onlookers.

With some commotion, Max and Beetle burst into the yard. Carrying a small wire cage, Max walked straight up to me and brandished the cage in my face. My face dropped in disbelief.

"That's not a mouse," I protested.

"Sure is, Spikey boy," replied Max.

"No, it's not. It's a rat."

"It's a big mouse," sneered Max.

"You've got to be jokin'. It's a rat."

"If I say it's a mouse, it's a mouse," Max taunted. "I've just fed him heaps."

"No, it's a rat," I repeated.

"No way, Spikey. Ya must be blind." His tone was dripping

in sarcasm. "Tell him what it is, Beetle. He doesn't seem to believe me."

"It's a big mouse," agreed Beetle.

I was wasting my time arguing. All the other kids remained silent as well. They had come to see a fight but were having mixed feelings now that they realised what Max was up to.

"Come on, Spike," Beetle quipped. "Ya can't chicken out now."

Max put his hand under his armpits and clucked and strutted around like a chook. They both laughed. They were obviously enjoying pushing me into this no-win situation.

My mind was searching for a way out. What could I do? Walter would be killed for sure.

"Walter will have to fight," whispered Leany. "They'll flippin' kill you if he doesn't."

The kids crowded around the drum. They believed I had no option but to sacrifice Walter. Max took his "mouse" from its little wire cage and carefully lowered it into the drum. I slowly lifted Walter from my pocket and looked at the rat ten times his size. I took in Walter's much smaller body and claws. I hated doing this. I couldn't stop the thought of the little mouse being ripped to pieces by a rat from filling my mind. My insides were churning. I wished I was home. I took a slow step towards the drum.

A voice broke the silence.

"Wait! Wait!"

I looked around. It was Snake.

"I'll be back in minute," he announced. "Don't start till I get back," he yelled, racing from the yard and down the footpath.

"Where's he goin'?" Max growled.

"He s-s-s-said s-s-s-something about g-g-g-getting h-his m-m-mouse," stuttered Sniff.

"Is he now," said Max. "Beauty. We'll have to wait till he gets back then. I hope he remembers to bring two bob with him." He smiled at Beetle and rubbed his hands together.

Snake was back in a flash, clutching a hessian bag. He looked at me and winked.

"I've got my mouse," he announced. "The three of them can fight."

He took his mouse from the bag.

"That's not a mouse," wailed Max.

"Yes, it is," replied Snake.

"It's a ferret!"

"No, it's not a ferret. It's a *big* mouse."

"It's a ferret. I know what a ferret looks like, you idiot," Max shouted.

"Open your eyes, Maxie," baited Snake. "It's a mouse."

"Mice don't grow that big," Max retorted.

"This one did. Should see what I feed him."

"Mice aren't that colour. It's yellow."

"Yeah," replied Snake. "Not many of 'em around these days."

From that moment, my opinion of Snake grew enormously. He had summed up the situation in a flash. He realised I had been forced into a corner by the two bullies and he didn't like it. More importantly, he was prepared to do something about it. He surprised me with his insight. He had more intuition and courage than I had ever given him credit for.

All the other kids were by now highly excited. The shoe was on the other foot and everyone was delighted. The expectation of the coming showdown unfolding as it was before them was beyond all imagination. Of course, Max and Beetle weren't very happy at all with the latest development. Max was becoming quite agitated.

"We're not fighting that thing," said Max, trying to regain control of the situation. "We're leavin'."

"No, you're not," threatened Snake. "You were going to force Spike to stay and fight. You're not going anywhere."

Max looked at Snake and knew he was serious. Snake was a real threat and this frightened him.

"Yeah, Max," someone called from the crowd. "You can't back out now."

Max swallowed hard. He picked up his rat from the drum and looked at it in the same way I had looked at Walter. The kids all crowded once again around the drum, although no one was too sure of what was going to happen.

Max continued to look at his rat. It was obvious to me that he didn't want it hurt.

"But I've had him for nearly a year. I don't want him killed," he said. His tough demeanour had melted away. He was subdued, shoulders slumped. "Mum gave him to me for my birthday. I don't want him hurt."

Beetle frowned and looked puzzled.

"You were going to kill Spike's mouse," said Snake. "You weren't too worried about that."

Max looked at me holding Walter in my hand.

"I'll tell you what, Spike," said Max. "Let's say you win the bet. I'll give you my two bob and we'll call it quits."

"No chance," said Snake. "You wanted a fight and you're going to get one."

"No!" pleaded Max. "He's the only pet I've ever had. He'll get killed."

"Okay," Snake conceded. "But everyone here came to see a fight. They're not going to be very happy if they miss out, are they?"

He handed Sniff his ferret and took off his jumper. He stared at Max, his blue eyes flashing.

"You and me, Maxie, or the three mice. Take your pick."

Max cringed, worry creasing his face. Snake was taller than him and appeared confident. For once, Max was scared. Picking on little kids was one thing; getting into a real fight with someone who could obviously look after himself was not something he cared to do. He clutched his rat, patting it gently on the head as he stared at Snake. He glanced back at the rat. He couldn't win, no matter what his decision was.

All the kids were still standing around the drum, but when Max sighed and put his rat gently into its wire cage, they spread out around the yard.

I could never see any sense in two kids trying to prove who was the best fighter. No one ever really got hurt and I don't think the kids fighting really wanted to hurt each other too badly anyway. But I had a feeling I was going to enjoy this one. A couple of wild swings from Max that missed by a mile, followed by two or three well placed whacks from Snake, and it was all over in a flash. Max, sporting a blood nose and swollen eye and clutching his rat in its wire cage, trudged off home with Beetle by his side. Snake with his ferret, Sniff, Leany and I with Walter tucked away in my pocket, walked towards our homes until we reached the step bridge where we went our separate ways.

I admired Snake. He didn't have a particularly happy home life and he was considered a bit of a dunce at school. But he was a likeable kid and, unless provoked, he wouldn't hurt a fly. More importantly, he had a mature sense of fair play, which became evident in later years when he developed into a champion athlete and sportsman. Although Snake never became one of my closest mates, we maintained a sort of bond. Because I was small and sometimes picked on by the occasional bully, I valued his friendship. I never had any more trouble with Max and Beetle; Snake had certainly put a stop to that.

Rooster Kid

Munro was not a big rooster, but he put the fear of God into all the neighbourhood kids. He was well known and his reputation as a ferocious fighter was widespread throughout the senior grades of my school. On many occasions, groups of excited kids would gather in our backyard and take part in one of their favourite pastimes – rooster racing.

Munro would be enticed to the centre of the ring and much baiting and teasing would be carried out to encourage the rooster to lose his cool and finally take off after the tormentor. An enthralling sprint to the gate would eventuate. This mad scramble was accompanied by shouts and cheers from the audience who adorned the shed roof and the woodpile. Usually, the five-second dash ended with the fleeing hero reaching the gate safely, although sometimes a scratch or two from Munro's beak or spurs was proudly displayed the next day at school.

How tough you were was measured by how close you would stand to Munro to begin the teasing ritual and how long you could stay there before fleeing to the safety of the gate. There was a real art in knowing when to run. You had to watch Munro's left eye. He always went through a routine before finally giving chase. His neck feathers would stand on end, one wing would slowly drop and his head would sag until his beak was a whisker from the ground, all while slowly rotating, soft, clicking noises echoing from deep within his throat like the ticking of a time bomb.

After a while, the left eye would suddenly close and all hell would break loose. As soon as the eyelid moved, you knew your time was up. You had a split second to turn and run as fast as you could to the gate, which was left strategically unlatched. Each contest was talked about for hours and at school the next day the whole episode was relived and exaggerated until it rivalled Bonaparte's Retreat.

Our backyard was an old-time adventure playground. No treated pine constructions like kids have nowadays but still as exciting. The yard was large with an assortment of old sheds; piles of firewood; a large, spreading peppercorn tree; a couple of fruit trees; and a henhouse. This henhouse was where the chooks slept and, because of the thick layer of chook dung on the floor, the shed was not a place to be frequented by any sane person. In fact, the chooks had the whole yard to themselves; it was their domain. Together with their dustbowls, feathers and droppings, they dominated the landscape. The whole place stank of chooks.

The worst feature, of course, was the multi-coloured chook dung that lay scattered on the dust around the yard. To be caught barefoot in this mini minefield was a frightening experience. Walking wasn't too bad. You had time to carefully pick your way through the dollops, plops and squirts. But running, as a lot of kids found out, was a task of precision. To change each stride in midair, at full pelt across the yard, was difficult. You had to, in your mind, calculate where your foot would land in four or five strides' time and hope like hell you were right. If not, you reached the gate with muck oozing from under your shoes or, worse still, from between your toes, and a quick trip to the tap was inevitable.

Cornelius Browning was a new boy at school, a strapping lad, large in both build and ego. His fair hair and big muscles were accompanied by a swollen head and an endless repertoire of fantastic feats that he made sure everyone knew about. He tried to convince us he had fought carpet snakes and even a python and had caught barracuda and sharks while holidaying in Hawaii.

"What about roosters?" said Leany one day as everyone listened for the fourteenth time to how Corny had tamed and milked a savage water buffalo near Darwin.

"Roosters?"

"Yeah. Roosters. Ever had a flippin' fight with a rooster?"

"A *rooster*?" repeated Corny. A look of disbelief came over his large, fair face. "A rooster? Are you serious? A piddlin' little rooster? God!"

"Munro would fix you right up," I said.

"Munro?"

"Yeah. Spike's rooster," continued Leany.

"How big's this rooster?" jeered Corny.

"'Bout that high," I said, holding my hand a foot from the ground.

Corny's face turned into a sneering smile. "Scared of a rooster? Hell, I once donged a mad emu with a fishin' rod – real big. He was gonna 'ave a go at m'dad. Frothin' at the beak he was. Fixed him up real good, I did."

"Munro can really fight," I said. "Can run fast too. You wouldn't dong him with a fishin' rod."

The challenge had been made. Corny glanced at the eager faces surrounding him and realised that there was no getting out of this one. He forced a smile.

"Where do ya live, Spike?"

"Near the railway line, over the step bridge," I said. "House with the blue roof. What about tonight after school?" I continued with a grin.

"Yeah, tonight," chorused the other kids excitedly.

The news of the scheduled contest between Corny and Munro spread quickly and soon the whole senior school was abuzz with excitement. Wherever I went, a small crowd of hangers-on surrounded me and offered suggestions as to how to psych Munro up to killer proportions.

"Tie razor blades on his spurs."

"Sharpen his beak."

"Give him a feed of Hypol. My mum says Hypol's good for ya. She says it makes you strong and puts hair on it."

Dad worked on the railways, shift work. He'd slept all afternoon and was getting ready to start at half past four when he looked out the kitchen window.

"Gawd! What's going on?"

There were kids everywhere. Every vantage point in the backyard was taken up, even the peppercorn tree was full of excited faces. Usually, the tree was not a favourite place because of the thick, smelly white sap that oozed from its trunk and branches, but today it was standing room only.

The chooks were rounded up and locked in the henhouse before Munro was coaxed into the arena with a few grains of wheat. The kids cheered and the rooster clucked, strutting proudly with an air of expectancy and looking around as if summing up the situation. The sun glistened on his iridescent feathers and flashes of red, orange, purple and aqua sliced through the dusty afternoon haze.

Another cheer erupted as Munro ruffled his neck feathers, stood on the tips of his toes and let forth a raucous crow.

During all this showmanship, Corny stared in amazement. He'd never seen or smelt a backyard like this before. In fact, he'd never seen anything *like this* before. He looked at the ground, screwed up his face and picked his way carefully between the chook droppings to the clearing. It reminded him of a film he'd seen a few weeks back about some people being pushed into an arena with a pack of hungry lions. They were quickly eaten while the spectators roared and cheered. Surely a rooster couldn't do much harm though. Corny couldn't remember anyone being killed and gobbled up by one.

"Got ya fishin rod, Corny?" yelled a kid on the shed roof.

Everyone roared and clapped and Corny waved half-heartedly. He was beginning to feel uneasy. He wasn't sure what he was supposed to do. How do you fight a rooster? How fast can they run?

While the rules were being explained to him, he was thinking quickly. If he was slick enough, he could grab the rooster by the neck or leg, swing it around and heave it over the fence. That would be impressive. The kids would think that was tops. He could even drop-kick it over the peppercorn tree. That'd be incredible. The kids would talk about it for months. Or he could even–

His thoughts were shattered when Munro stood on tiptoe again and crowed to the spectators roaring their approval.

"Come on, Munro!"

"Show him, Munro!"

"Stick ya spurs into his bum, Munro!"

That remark brought forth a roar of laughter and the kids in the peppercorn tree almost fell to the ground in their efforts to hold on and laugh at the same time.

While the audience settled down, I took the time to niggle Munro. I flicked my hand at him a few times and stamped my foot near him in the dust. His feathers ruffled and his wings drooped. It was time for me to scram. This left Corny and Munro eyeing each other off. A hush fell over the crowd.

At this stage, Corny was still some distance from the rooster, who was alternating slowly from one foot to the other. His neck feathers stood on end and his head was sinking slowly to the ground. Corny edged closer, deciding to snatch at the rooster's extended neck. He would grab, drop and kick all in one action. He edged closer still. He was close enough now. The spectators held their breath. Munro clicked softly. If television had been around in those days, the action that followed would have been shown in slow motion on *World of Sport*.

The whole yard erupted. The kids roared and the dust swirled.

Corny's problem was that just as Munro's left eyelid shut, somebody in the peppercorn tree lost their footing, slipped and got sap on their new shorts.

"Hell, Mum'll kill me," a voice wailed.

Unfortunately, Corny glanced up and was immediately smashed in the chest by a ball of shiny fighting feathers.

Corny's breath burst from his lungs and the force of the onslaught knocked him backwards onto the ground. Munro had never had it so good; never before had anyone been in this position. Corny raised himself on all fours, his stomach pointing to the sky, and tried to scrabble backwards like an upside-down crab. Munro sprang into the air and landed on a protruding knee. Corny lashed out with the other leg. The rooster jumped to avoid it and landed on Corny's chest. Corny let out a screech and again shot backwards on all fours, his face a picture of fear. Munro ripped at his checked shirt with beak and spurs.

The crowd was hysterical, their yelling and cheering heard on the other side of the railway line. During Munro's attack, Corny was making high-pitched whimpering sounds and was still making his way towards the gate on his hands and heels. A track had been scraped through the dust and dung and Corny was covered in a layer of smelly muck.

All this was too much for the woodpile. The stakes holding the rows of wood suddenly gave way and a sea of arms, legs, heads and foot blocks spilled out into the clearing. Munro took fright and jumped high into the air. Corny, taking advantage of the sudden calamity, jumped to his feet and was about to take refuge when he was struck from behind by a piece of rolling wood, landing him flat on his stomach. At the same time, the rooster regained his composure and, having eyes only for the checked shirt, landed, ripping and tearing, on Corny's back.

The boy reacted savagely. He swung his arms wildly, struggled to his knees and tried to grab Munro by the neck. The rooster jumped on top of Corny's head, grabbed a beak full of hair and held on with his claws like a water skier.

The gate was only a few yards off and all efforts were now

concentrated on reaching it. The kids who were scattered from the woodpile had now congregated along the middle fence, their bruises and scratches forgotten for the moment. Corny had given up trying to free himself from the rooster and was crawling through the dollops to the gate with Munro still tugging savagely on his fair hair.

The kids cheered when Corny clawed his way to the wooden palings of the gate and rattled it vigorously. The latch on the other side of the gate, however, was still on. Corny slumped to the ground and lay sobbing, the rooster standing triumphantly on his head.

The crowd hushed. The peppercorn tree grew silent. Some of the kids looked at me. I climbed down from the vantage point on the shed and ran to the crumpled heap near the gate. At the same time, Munro sensed the change in the action and jumped to the ground, strands of hair hanging from his beak. He strutted from the scene and disappeared round the corner of the henhouse.

With my help, Corny slowly raised himself to a kneeling position and remained there for a while, tears rolling down his grimy face. He was a real mess, covered with dust and smears and streaks of chook dung. His shirt was shredded in places, and it did nothing to hide the red scratches on his back and chest. He clambered to his feet and stood shaking while the other kids crowded around.

Corny looked at them through blurred eyes. His head and shoulders hung low. The kids quietly observed the miserable figure.

"Good on ya, Corny," said someone softly.

"Yeah! Ya almost made it."

"We told ya Munro was vicious."

Corny didn't lift his head. I undid the latch on the gate. He turned and laboured from the backyard, plodding up the brick path to where his bike leant against the tin fence. He tucked his filthy trousers into his socks, jumped on and headed down the road towards the railway line. The kids stood quietly in little groups discussing the episode. Then they filtered off to their own homes.

Corny wasn't at school the next day. In fact, he was not seen until the following Monday. When he returned, nothing was said to him about the event. We felt we didn't need to.

But that didn't stop the story from being told and retold for months. Even Dad, who had watched the whole thing from over the back fence on his way to work, often asked how the rooster kid was and went off chuckling to himself.

Dickie Larsen's Pumpkin

An annual event that was held with much ceremony at our church was the harvest. Thanksgiving. The congregation would bring along produce from their gardens that would in turn be donated to the local hospital to feed and brighten up the patients. A wide variety of fresh fruit and vegetables, bunches of flowers, eggs, honey, jams and preserves would be brought along early to church on one particular Sunday morning and arranged on a long trestle erected especially for this special occasion. Bert the minister would bless the harvest and thank everyone for their generosity. Later that day, the whole lot would be packed into boxes and delivered to the hospital.

Everyone felt good and important and for once the church appeared a little happier and brighter, the gloom diminished by the colours and smells of the fresh food and flowers.

Dad always had a large vegetable garden at home, as did most people in those days. It was only on rare occasions that Mum had to buy anything from the greengrocer or visit the local Chinese market garden. Along with twenty or so fruit trees and grapevines, we were very well provided for and largely self-sufficient. Dad spent a great deal of time tending his garden and was always very proud of the results.

The pumpkin patch was situated in the backyard where there was plenty of room for them to spread. This area was surrounded by a wire fence that kept the chooks from pecking at the pumpkins and scratching around the plants. The large yellow flowers would appear amongst the leaves during late spring and the little green pumpkins would begin to grow at the base of these flowers.

When the flowers died and the little pumpkins were about the size of tennis balls, it was usual for each kid to write their name on a particular one. The name was scratched around the middle of the pumpkin with a sharp stick or a nail. The letters would usually stretch right around the little pumpkin. As the pumpkin grew and slowly changed colour, the written names would grow as well. When the pumpkin was fully grown, the letters stood out boldly against the yellow or grey skins of the pumpkins. Our named pumpkin was regarded as our own and it was quite exciting to finally break it from the plant and store it in the cellar to be eaten at a later date. Quite a few kids from the neighbourhood would write their names on Dad's pumpkins as well. Dad didn't seem to mind and would sometimes give the grown pumpkin to them as a gift anyway. The Larsen boys, Ernie and Dickie, who lived on the opposite corner to us, were two who always made a point of scratching their names on a pumpkin, probably hoping it would be theirs to keep when they were ready to eat.

On the Saturday before the Thanksgiving harvest, Dad and I climbed down the steps into the dimly lit cellar and collected an assortment of vegetables, bottles of preserved fruit, jars of honey and a couple dozen eggs. All were put into cardboard boxes or hessian bags, carted up the steps and stored on the back verandah to be packed in the car the next morning.

We arrived at the church earlier than usual that Sunday morning. We carted all the boxes and bags through the back door and left them near the long trestle that had been covered with white linen tablecloths. It was the task of a few volunteers to arrange everything on and around the trestle before the church service began.

Gradually, the congregation filled the church while the volunteers completed the mammoth job of placing all the produce in position. The display looked wonderful. All the larger items – pumpkins, melons and bags of potatoes – had been placed on the bottom of the pile. All the smaller pieces of fruit and vegetables were somehow arranged on top of them. Along the front of the trestle was a row of hay bales on which most of the jars and bottles were stacked on top of the larger ones. Eggs were on display in wire egg baskets hanging from special wooden stands at intervals along the trestle. The flowers were arranged in buckets and large vases and at each end of the display were sheaves of wheat and barley leaning against each other so that they stood nearly as high as the produce on the trestle. The entire show was quite impressive. The varied colours produced something vibrant and real; when you closed your eyes and took a deep breath, you could smell the flowers and the fruit and the hay. The church was transformed into something that reminded me of warm days in the bush, picnics and having fun with my friends as we played in the garden.

It was usual for us kids to sit in the front two rows every Sunday and remain in the church until the minister completed the first half of the service. When the children's story was finished, we would all stand up and file from the church, leaving the adults to endure the remainder of the session and Bert's sermon.

Everyone was in a rather light-hearted mood this particular day. They all felt good knowing that they were helping the sick people in the hospital. The local newspaper would no doubt run a story about the generous and hardworking churchgoers and photos of the mountain of donations and a sick patient or two would grace the front page. The special guests, Dr James and the boss of the hospital, stood and smiled when Bert introduced them to everyone. It was going to be a memorable day. In fact, it was going to be a day that everyone remembered for a long, long time!

The service had just begun when a couple of girls in the front row started to giggle. One of them whispered something to the boy beside her and it wasn't long before the whole front row was squirming in muffled hysterics. They were trying to control themselves; this wasn't really the place to be behaving in such a disruptive manner. But they were fighting a losing battle. I was in the second row, feeling quite embarrassed by the antics of the kids in front of me. But it wasn't long before the second row got wind of the cause of the hilarity.

Ernie Larsen erupted in the seat beside me, pointing to the vegetables on the trestle. It was his brother's big yellow pumpkin that Dad had unknowingly brought to the church that was the centre of all the attention. His name had been written on the pumpkin months before. The large letters now stood out boldly against the coloured skin. The problem was that the first and the last letters of his surname were hidden around the sides of the pumpkin, leaving the rest of the word in full view.

It's very difficult not to laugh when everyone around you is splitting their sides. We were in church, where this sort of thing was definitely outlawed. But laughter really is infectious, and the kids had resorted to all sorts in their endeavour to be as normal as they could. At various times, it seemed that the raucous behaviour was dying down, but as soon as someone looked at the pumpkin, control was again lost and a chain reaction once again set in. Some of the kids seemed like they were internally haemorrhaging in their efforts not to explode in loud laughter, while others had bright red faces and tears streaming down their cheeks. Little Willy Watts wet himself. Poor old Bert didn't know what was going on. He was in the pulpit at the side of the display and couldn't see the offending pumpkin. He continued on bravely, frowning as he glared menacingly at the kids convulsing in the front two rows.

Old Mrs Cornes played the organ every Sunday. The giant pipe organ had to be pumped by foot in order to force air into the pipes. This in turn created the music. The large, wide pedal at the base squeaked as it went up and down. It was a real effort for Mrs Cornes to work the pedals; the music ebbed and flowed with her energy levels. Occasionally, when she felt inspired, she gave the pedal a real working over, which rattled the vase of flowers and shook the two candles that sat at each end of the organ. But right now, Mrs Cornes was becoming increasingly wild at the kids still finding the pumpkin a source of great amusement. The rest of the congregation shuffled restlessly in their seats as well. Some of the adults were by now aware of the problem but didn't know quite what to do about it.

Old Mrs Cornes knew what to do. While Bert continued to warble about building on the rock and not on the sand, his favourite children's story that we'd heard a thousand times, she quietly rose from her stool, creeping towards the pumpkin, music book clutched in hand. Everyone watched her as she reached the pumpkin and gingerly placed the book in front of it. Glancing triumphantly at the red faces in the front two rows and happy with her courageous effort, she nonchalantly crept back to the organ, trying to ignore the fact that she was the centre of attention.

With a thick thud, the book slipped and fell on top of some jars of beetroot that were clustered on a hay bale. All the kids erupted once again. Mrs Cornes stopped in her tracks. All eyes were on her as she once more tiptoed towards the pumpkin. Bert stopped preaching, his gaze catching on the hunched figure of Mrs Cornes, his face an expression of confusion. Silence fell over the congregation as everyone tried to guess what Mrs Cornes would do next. This time she decided to grab the pumpkin and slowly turn it around so that the offending word could no longer be seen. This proved to be more difficult than she realised because of all the other fruit and vegetables that were piled on top of it. Her face strained as she struggled to move the large pumpkin.

Everyone held their breath. Gradually, the yellow pumpkin rotated until the word that had caused so much disruption was out of sight. But when the kids saw the part of the boy's first name that was now on show, all hell broke loose. Although not a very rude word, it was the straw that broke the camel's back. This was beyond any self-control and all the kids and even a few adults just couldn't cope. There was an immediate uproar. Caution was thrown to the wind. Church or no church, this was a classic. Kids were rolling around in hysterics, tears streaming down red faces. Willy Watts wet himself again. Mrs Cornes was mortified. Mustering unknown strength, she snatched at the pumpkin and wrenched it from its resting place.

But this had a terrible effect on the mountain of produce on the trestle. At first a few apples and peaches rolled from the top and plonked onto the floor. A lettuce gave way and knocked over an egg stand, which in turn had a snowball effect on the rest of the pile. In an instant, produce went everywhere. An avalanche of eggs, fruit, vegetables, jars, bottles, bags of potatoes and onions all crashed to the floor. The sound of smashing eggs and breaking glass was heard above the squelching and thuds of the rest of the debris. Poor old Mrs Cornes tried valiantly to escape the terrible onslaught only to have her legs knocked from beneath her by a monstrous watermelon that bounced off her and crashed into the organ. The vase of flowers on the organ crashed to the floor. One of the candles teetered for a few seconds, hot wax spilling down its sides, before it fell and rolled towards the sheaves of wheat. Mrs Cornes lay stretched out on the floor, clutching at the candle as it rolled by. But her efforts failed, and the wheat burst into flames, the bales of hay and white tablecloths catching alight as well.

It was in this moment that the kids in the front rows decided that they'd seen enough for one day. They scrambled up the aisles and burst from the front door of the church, most of the adults not far behind them. Some of the men ran to get buckets of water to throw on the fire. A white and shaken Mrs Cornes staggered from the church and collapsed into the arms of the first person she saw. Someone who was still able to think contacted the fire brigade, but by the time they arrived, the damage had been done. The wooden floor was burning ferociously and eventually it collapsed in a shower of sparks and smoke. The whole Thanksgiving harvest disappeared down the gaping hole and came to rest on the ground beneath the church. Jars and bottles were exploding in the heat and the fruit and vegetables were sizzling and bubbling. On the top of everything sat the organ, flames belching from its wooden frame and padded stool. Outside, everyone watched the smoke pouring from the air vents and doors and the few open windows. Firemen were spraying water on the flames.

The local newspaper ran the story of the fire on the front page. The damage, it claimed, was caused by a candle that had accidentally fallen onto a sheaf of wheat. No mention was made of Dickie Larsen's pumpkin or Mrs Cornes' ordeal. For the next couple of months, all the church services were held in the Sunday school hall while repairs were carried out. The whole building was painted and a new wooden floor installed. Much to Mrs Cornes' pleasure, a brand-new organ was purchased. This one didn't have to be pumped, and candles were never, ever seen on it. Over the years, we continued to scratch our names on the little pumpkins. Dad never stopped us, but he did encourage Ernie and Dickie to write their initials only, standing watch in case they got over-enthusiastic. Despite the damage to the church, I think underneath it all, Dad saw the funny side of the whole episode. But, of course, he never, ever let on.

Acknowledgements

Thank you to my children and many grandchildren for their help and encouragement in the completion of this book.

To Narelle, who worked hard on limited time to compile the manuscript ready for publication as well as Andrew, Melinda and Peter for their later support in bringing this book to reality. Thank you, too, to my dear wife Sherree for her advice and patience.

And finally, memories are still vivid of my childhood mates – Leany and Riddy – not here to read the shenanigans in writing but who live on in the stories I have written ...

About the Author

Geoffrey Carr grew up in the Wimmera town of Stawell and cherished his caring and loving childhood, enveloped in the blue silhouettes of the famous Grampians and lesser-known Black Ranges of the region. This was the setting before commencing his teaching career and settling in the Ballarat region for over fifty years. Although living in Ballarat and raising six children there, he has spent that whole time being drawn back to the region he grew up in and the bush he loved – whether it be for the Easter Stawell Gift, family Christmases, rabbiting in the bush with his dad, lazy summers at Lake Fyans or earlier years fishing at Lake Lonsdale. With both his parents' families originating across Pomonal, Great Western, Stawell and Ballarat, he is truly a "gentle"man that believes home is where the heart is and there's always time for a good cheeky yarn.

The Originals

The following pages contain the scans of some of the original stories as handwritten by Geoffrey Carr at the time of writing. Working closely with his daughter, Narelle, these handwritten pages became digital, leading eventually to this very book you hold in your hands.

OUR HOUSE

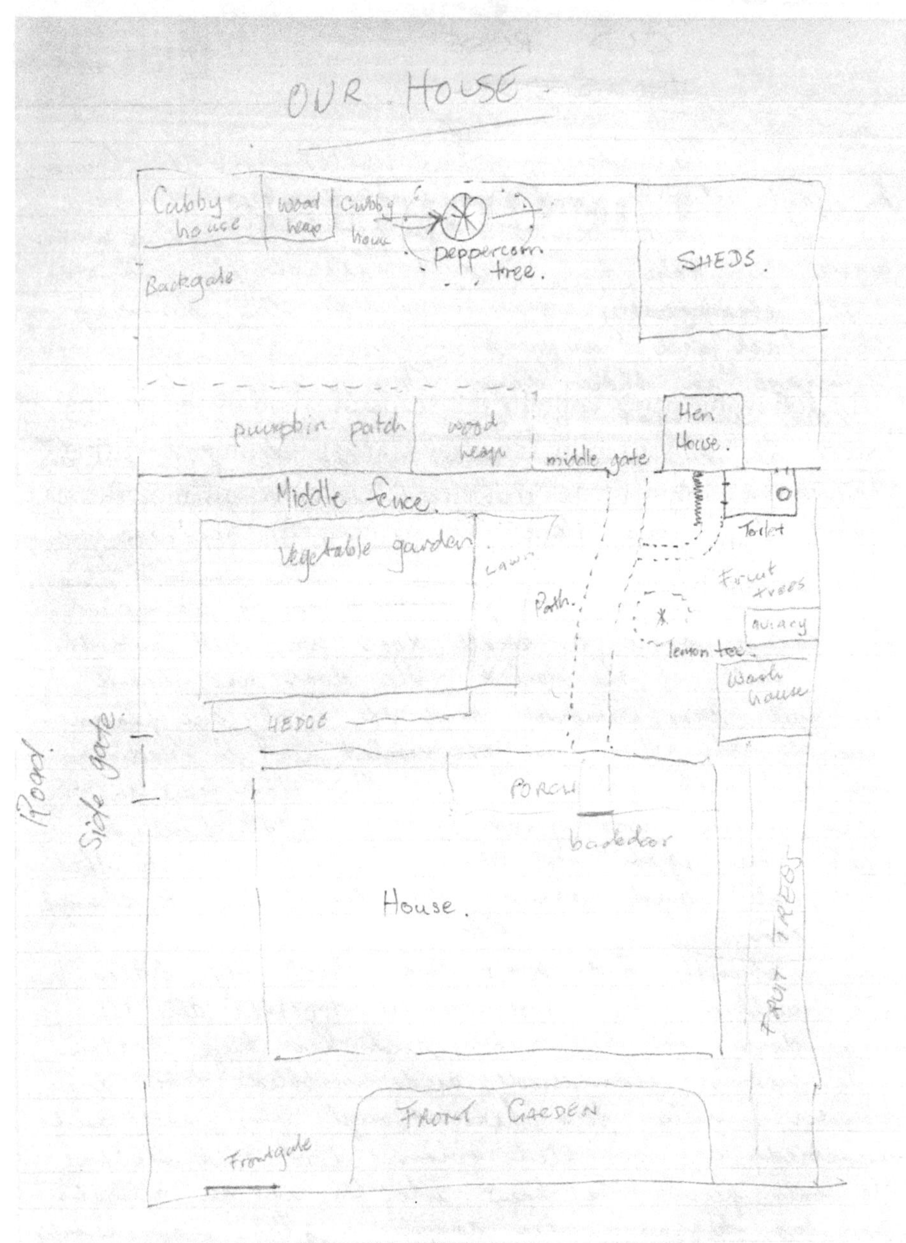

the front of the cart. Got ya' whip?"
Snuff fumbled around the floor of the chariot
and held up a thin stick with a small
leather strap attached to the end.
"Y-y y, y yeh," he stuttered.
"Okay," yelled kiddy, appointing himself the
official starter. "Get ready."
The crowd hushed.
"Go."

I was about to relax in the warmth of the
sun again when suddenly the dog shot to his feet
and let out an almighty yelp. He took off
round the house shaking his head and pawing
at his mouth with his front feet. All the time
he was whimpering and whining. I watched
in astonishment as he raced back onto the
verandah, hurtled three times round the rocking
chair and headed for his tin of water
under the lemon tree. I didn't think a dog
Honk's size could drink so much water but
finally he lifted his head and flopped down
on the dirt panting.
I took another seed

There was a real art in knowing
when to run. You had to keep your
eye on Munro's left eye. He went
through a routine before he
finally chase. His neck feathers would
stand on end, one wing would drop
and his head would sag until
his beak was a whisker from the ground.
And All the time he would slowly
rotate, soft clicking noises
echoed from deep in his throat like the
ticking of a clock. And he never took

OLD ROSE

~~the D.C.M.~~

Our toilet seemed miles from the house.
In fact Uncle Ivan said that when he visited
us he always brought a cut lunch and a water
bottle in case he needed to take the trip. It was
built ~~thoughtfully~~ along the fence line dividing
the back yard and the house yard. c/o
sewerage in those days. Once a week, whether
needed or not, a poor old man would come
with an pan, and replace the full one.

Old Bert had been the local minister
for many, many years. He rode an old brown
big bicycle and always wore a pair of silver
bicycle clips to stop his black pants from
getting caught in the chain. He was a tiny
little bloke with a sandy complexion and
a weather beaten face. But the main feature
of his nut like head was a huge set of buck
teeth which protruded at an unfortunate angle
from between his lips. They were so big and
stuck out so far that he could never
close his mouth properly. Dad said that
Old Bert had been known to eat an apple
through a tennis racquet.

To my kids who were ~~not~~ born too late.

The Fifties
Life was simple then.
Simple, but exciting and wholesome.
Dad went to work each day.
~~And at home~~ Cut the wood
Grew vegetables and flowers
Fed the chooks and dogs and ferrets
And had a drink every pay day at the Pub.
Mum stayed home
And cooked and cleaned and sewed
Did the shopping once a week.

Credits

Editor

Anna Bilbrough of Coven Press

Artistic Credits

Internal illustrations by Elizabeth McCracken
and Stephanie Talevski of Coven Press

Cover Designer

Elizabeth McCracken of Coven Press
Designer and illustrator

Internal Formatting

Alana Lambert of Coven Press
Headings: Lavigne Text/28pt
Body: Adobe Caslon Pro/12pt/16pt leading